D-City
Chronicles
Aja & Ro
Book One

A Novel by
Annitia L. Jackson

To submit a manuscript for our review, email us at

submissions@majorkeypublishing.com

Be sure to LIKE our Major Key Publishing

page on Facebook!

Acknowledgments

I would like to dedicate this book to my grandmother Hattie Fletcher. She is my guardian angel in heaven. She taught me to follow my dreams I will always be indebted to her for that. Love you, Mama!

This book was a long time coming. I just want to take this time to say thanks to my husband Ron Jackson for encouraging me and having my back while I took a step out on faith. Thank you for being an amazing father to our son Nathan and keeping his five year old energy at bay while I put pen to paper. You are my soulmate and helped me to understand what real love is. I love you and Nathan to the moon and beyond.

I want to also thank my middle school teacher Barbara Middlebrooks for introducing me to writing. You woke up a fire in me that I never knew existed.

To my personal reading crew Zeanola, Undrea, Shawauna, Diedra, Kimessia, and Marcia that would definitely share their opinions both good and bad, I want to thank you for helping me. I love you ladies so much!!

I would also like to thank my sister Kasandra, my cousin Ingrid, and my nephew Robert. You guys are my inspiration for going after my dream of being an author. I have watched you all accomplish your goals and it inspired me.

And to my riders who always have my back Renee and Freda, I love you both so much.

Chapter 1- Aja

I can't believe this is happening to me! The last thing I remember is walking home from school with my boyfriend Desmond. Now here I am handcuffed to a canopy bed dressed in an expensive silk white gown. I woke up three hours ago to this nightmare wondering where I am and where the hell is Desmond.

I moved to my side as much as I could with the handcuffs because my back was starting to hurt from laying on it for so long. What did I do to deserve this! I am nobody special, I'm just Aja Lanae Masters that lived in D- City projects.

I've lived there all of my 16 years of life with my alcoholic mother April, my little sister Akia and my older brother Ace. My mama April lived for her Gin and nothing else. I remember growing up with the lights being turned off every other month and eating whatever WIC or whatever the food bank provided. Let's just say that my relationship with her was fucked up.

My big brother Ace was more of our parent. He is 21 and started slinging at

14 just so we could eat and keep a roof over our heads. His mentor Calvin better known as Big C stepped down and handed him D-City to run. I know he is tearing up the streets looking for me. Ace was imposing in his own right just by his size. He stood 6'2 225 pounds of pure muscle. He was honey color with long dreadlocks tipped with red. He has the blackest eyes you have ever seen and a scar on his face going from his scalp to his chin that gave him a dangerous look.

My sister Akia was taller than me at 5'8 and slim thick with a head full of curls she kept cut in a bob. Akia is the color of coffee with cream and has cat like eyes. She is 15 and is full of fire. She is always getting in fights but she is my heart. I would go to war for her and my brother and I know they would do the same for me. I was the opposite of Akia. I went to school, made good grades, and kept my head down. A lot of people call me shy because I don't talk a lot but I am far from it. I just don't deal with people because they are fake and always let you down. I learned that from my no good mama and nonexistent daddy. My sister, brother, and my girl Kyra were my best friends.

I'm cute, I'm not going to front. I'm 5'7 with shoulder length hair and a milk chocolate complexion with big brown eyes that everyone seemed to love. I'm thick weighing 160 in all the right places. Men and boys were always trying to get at me but I never paid them any attention.

Desmond was lucky I even messed with him. He was one of my brother's best friends and after asking me out for months I finally said yes. We have been dating for over 3 months now and he was an okay boyfriend plus he was fine as hell. He was milk chocolate 6 feet even with an athletic build. Dark brown eyes and a killer smile that made me melt.

Where is he? I thought as my mind took me back on our conversation while walking away from school.

"Desmond, I told you I'm just not ready to take it there with you. I've never had sex and I don't plan on it anytime soon." He looked at me with a scowl on his face.

"Why you acting like I just want to hit and walk away! I'm your man and you should want to satisfy my needs!" I looked up at him like he had lost his mind. *Was he really yelling at me like he doesn't have any sense? Oh hell naw!!!*

"Let me tell you something, first of all you need to bring it all the way down when you are talking to me. Second, just because I'm your girl

doesn't mean you can demand to have sex with me anytime you want! I told you I'm not ready!!"

He was about to say something else when a van skidded to a halt right in front of us. Three men jumped out with mask on and grabbed Desmond and me. I tried to fight back but the guy that had me put a cloth over my mouth and everything turned black.

That's the last time I saw Desmond. Tears were running down my face and the tightness in my chest was like a vise grip. Where was I? Where is Desmond, and what in the hell is going on? As soon as I was thinking it, the locks on the door turned and little did I know my nightmare was about to begin.

Desmond

What the fuck is going on!!! I was walking down the street talking to Aja and some men jumped out of the van and grabbed us. I tried to run but those mutherfuckers hit me in the head with a gun knocking me out. I woke up about an hour ago tied to this nasty ass bed. I hope my brother Derrick is looking for me.

I was supposed to give him an update on getting close to Aja so we could set up her brother Ace and kill him. I know I was shady as fuck since he's supposed to be my friend but, I was tired of getting the scraps. See my twin brother Derrick and I had been plotting for a couple of years on how to get rid of Ace but he was always two steps ahead of us. I was his friend but hell he didn't trust me with shit and I needed to know who his connect was.

One day I saw him in the mall with his two sisters and I saw how he was with them. I knew the best way to get to him was through them. I picked Aja because she was quiet and I figured I could control her. Plus she was fine as hell and I wanted to hit that but the bitch was stingy as hell with giving it up.

I wasn't hurting I had five others on my roster that was fucking and sucking me whenever I wanted including my two baby mamas. I just wanted some of that tight ass virgin pussy Aja had. Fuck her teasing ass!!! I just need to find a way to get out of here. I hope her brother didn't find out about my brother and me.

I started hearing voices that sounded like Aja and some dude talking. I tried to lean over to hear what they were saying and the next thing I heard was her screams coming down towards my door.

Unknown

I walked in and looked at my angel lying there in the bed. She was flawless.

Beautiful chocolate skin, big thick thighs showing where the white gown I bought her had ridden up, with those eyes that have mesmerized me since the beginning.

She was looking at me with tears in those same eyes shaking with fear. I would never hurt her. She meant everything to me, hell she was my everything. She was going to be my wife as soon as she turned 18. She didn't know that just yet but I have known she would be my queen since she was ten years old.

I remember the day my heart was taken. I was in D-City handling some business when I saw a little girl walking with her mama across the basketball court. I had originally zoomed in on her mama who was fine as hell but when I got to her face I could tell she was drunk which was a huge turn off. She was walking fast as hell like she had somewhere to be. The lady was walking so fast that the little girl tripped and fell but her mama kept walking.

I went over to help her up and that's when our eyes met. Her big brown eyes looked into my soul and I was hooked. I felt some kind of way because here

I'm thirty-seven years old looking at a ten year old but it wasn't sexual it was deeper than that. From that day on I followed her and learned everything I could about her until now.

I was waiting for her to turn eighteen so she could be mine. She was a good girl. Smart as hell, beautiful face, nice body, and she wasn't a hoe like her mama or these other ones running around here. I knew she was created just for me. My perfect Angel. She was saving herself for me I could tell. I wanted her to finish school before I made her mine completely so I fell back and just watched.

That was until he came along and fucked up everything! He wanted my pure angel and that was not happening. I had to get him away from her before he ruined her. I got information on him too his name was Desmond and he was no good for her. Little did she know he had girls all over the city and 2 babies that he didn't take care of. He was beneath her and I had to stop this relationship they had before it was too late. I was only going to kill him but I had to let Aja know that I was the only one for her and nobody else period.

I didn't want her to see my other side until I claimed her and made her mine but this mutherfucker got in my way. I was a King and he was a fucking peasant in the way of me getting my queen so he had to die.

I walked over to her and sat down on the bed. I still had my mask on because I wasn't ready for her to know me just yet. I know I have to wait to fully have her until she is eighteen but I just need to touch her so I can make it through. She flinched as soon as I started running my fingers through her silky black hair.

"Please don't hurt me!" she said in a shaky voice.

I was offended that she didn't see the love in my eyes for her but I checked my temper because she was innocent and didn't know the look of a man in love.

"My angel I would never hurt you. You belong to me and I will always treasure you." I said trying to reassure her.

"Where's Desmond? Why did you take us?" she asked with tears rolling down her soft cheek.

My darkness threatened to take over when she mentioned his damn name.

Fuck him! He was a boy and I'm a man.

"Don't ever mention another man's name! You belong to me! You want him!! Let me show you what happens to people who try and take what's mine!"

I unlocked the cuffs and threw her over my shoulder.

"Stop please I'm sorry!!! Put me down!" Aja cried.

I said nothing as I opened the door and walked down the hallway with her over my shoulder. I came to the end of the hallway and opened the doorway to the place I had fuck boy tied up in. I put her down and she ran right to the mutherfucker.

"Desmond!!! Are you okay?" she took the sock out of his mouth and untied his hands.

"I'm okay baby girl are you alright? What did he do to you?" he looked at her and touched her face and asked like I would hurt my queen.

This was making me sick watching him touch her. Fuck this playtime was over!

"Get your fucking hands off my girl!!! I pulled out my machete I had hidden behind the dresser.

Both their eyes got big. He pushed Aja away from him and held his hands up.

"Man I don't want any problems! Look you can have that bitch!!! I don't want her anyway!! Just let me go and I won't tell anybody! He cried like the little bitch he was.

I noticed he was peeing on himself as he was talking. I looked over at my angel and she had a look of disbelief on her face at the words he was speaking.

"Really Desmond?!" Are you kidding me!!!" she screamed.

"Fuck him angel he was never good enough for you anyway."

I lunged at him and started hacking at his neck with the machete until his head rolled off. Blood was everywhere and my angel was covered in it and screaming.

"Oh my God noooooooooooooooooooooo!!!!!!" she broke down and was lying on the floor crying.

I dropped the machete and picked my angel up and took her to the room and locked the door behind me putting the key in my pocket. I placed her gently on the toilet in the bathroom while I started the shower. Once the water was hot like she liked it I placed her under the water and grabbed the Dove body wash that she liked to use. I have watched her shower numerous times thanks to the hidden cameras I had installed at her mama's house. I washed her up making sure no blood remained on her beautiful body and dried her off. I picked her up and took her to the bed and laid her down gently and covered her with a new silk gown.

I wanted her so bad but it was not the time to claim her. I just needed a taste. She was zoned out in shock and I had to make her feel better. I eased her legs apart and looked at her pretty ass treasure. It was pink and wet from the shower. I bent my head down and inhaled her sweet scent. Just one taste and I knew I could make both of us feel better. I licked her slowly from front to back and started sucking on her button. She tried to move away but I clamped down hard on her thighs I know she would have bruises but I needed her to know I could make her feel good.

Her body started getting wetter and I knew she was close to her first ever climax and I was the first one to make her feel this way. I would be her only one.

She was crying and screaming no but it didn't matter she would get used to my touch. She came in my mouth and laid there with a defeated look on her face with tears and snot running down her cheeks.

"Angel you taste so good! I know it was your first time and you were nervous. It will get even better once I claim you. I'm going to let you rest and I will take you home after you wake up. Just know that you are mine and I will make you my wife as soon as you turn 18." I said standing up and rubbing her sweet juices from my lips.

I was brick hard and didn't want to scare her so I shifted away from her. I watched her until she fell asleep crying. I put her original clothes on her that she wore to school and put her in the van. I took her to the park by the school and placed her gently on the bench. I laid a red rose beside her with a note.

It said, *I will be back for you my angel when you turn 18.No one will ever come between us or they will die. Love, your everything. P.S. I will always be watching.*

I called the police on my burner phone to let them know where my angel was. I didn't want anything to happen to her. I left the van there with Desmond's hacked up body in it. I also told the police about him. This would be a warning to all who tried to come between us. I blended into the shadows as I heard the sirens. But, I would never be far from my Angel Aja.

Chapter 2- Ace

Four years later

"Shut the fuck up!! Where the hell is my money, Tavis?" I said smacking the shit out of my soon to be former driver.

"Ace man I promise I dropped the money off just like you said! Calvin and

Akia were there and took the bag. They counted it and everything just talk to them please!!" he begged.

I pulled my 9 millimeter about to light his lying ass up when my partners Ro and his brother Raymond walked through the door.

I met Ro and Raymond through their father Rodney who was my connect.

Raymond was my right hand and Ro was my enforcer. We all equally ran the D-

City Boyz. We had our hand in drugs, guns, hits, and credit card fraud. You name it we made money off of it. When we hooked up two years ago I was pissed Rodney wanted his sons to take over his part of the business. We had a good system going. But once I met them and seen they were about business we became unstoppable as business partners and brothers.

"Man Ace what you got Tavis all bloody for? You know his mama gonna be mad you made him mess up his school clothes! He said sitting down at the desk in the room.

"This mutherfucker lost five thousand dollars of our money." I said mushing

Tavis in the head.

Ro slowly walked over to Tavis with a smile on his face. I know that smile and I immediately get chills. See Ro is crazy literally. He never smiled unless he was killing or torturing someone. He has blackouts as he calls them and when he does he changes to a totally different person. He won't speak at all and the person he targets during his episodes is in for a world of pain. No one can bring him out of them but his dad. I ain't a scary nigga but I don't fuck with him when he gets like that.

The first time I saw him black out he took a spoon and dug this fiend's eye out for trying to sell his mama's wheelchair. Nigga had mama issues ever since his mama was murdered 3 years ago.

"So you like to steal Tavis?" Ro asked in a low voice.

"Naw Ro man I promise the money was all there when I dropped it off!!"

Tavis yelled as tears ran down his face.

Ro walked away from Tavis shaking his head and going over to the closet that was in the room.

He reached in and got out a wrench and walked over to

Tavis with that evil ass grin.

"Tavis I just bought this nice ass white Gucci shirt and you about to make me fuck it up. Now one more time where is the money." He said in a deadly calm.

Tavis started crying harder with snot running out his nose dripping everywhere.

"Okay please kill me fast Ace don't let that crazy ass mutherfucker near me and I will tell you where the money is!" Tavis screamed.

He was terrified shaking and shit and I loved every minute.

"Alright talk!" I screamed.

"Look I got behind on my child support payments and they were talking about locking me up and I needed the money. You know my ex is a bitch! I told her when she left me I wasn't given her no more money and she filed them papers on me! It's not my fault man. I didn't want all them damn kids anyway!" he said like that was something I should sympathize with.

This stupid ass nigga used to beat on his girlfriend and they have 3 kids together. She finally got some sense and left his stupid ass and now he wants to be a deadbeat ass mutherfucker. This situation was dead once I heard him say my money was gone. So, that meant his ass was about to be gone. I turned to

Raymond and motioned for him to come outside with me so we could light one up. This shit had stressed me out plus I knew shit was about to get real.

"Ro I'll buy you a new shirt." I said as I walked out I didn't even have to look back to know that it was about to get bloody.

Ro

I stepped out of the shower and grabbed the towel that was hanging on the door and wrapped it around my waist. I walked over to the mirror and wiped it off and took a look at my face in the mirror to make sure I got all the blood off of me.

My name is Roland Symir Casey but everyone calls me Ro. I'm 6'5 and weigh 240 pounds worth of muscles with a chocolate complexion. I have low cut wavy hair I got from my Mama and light brown eyes. I don't have any facial hair and have only one tattoo on my body which is a viper on my right arm. I'm 25 years old and have a little brother named Raymond who's 20.

My father is Big Rodney he runs the state of Tennessee. You name it he has his hands in it and makes millions. He taught me everything I know on how to move in silence. See everyone sees me as the enforcer for the D-City Boyz but what they don't know is that I'm a professional hit man called Viper.

I always have been good at killing and have had violent tendencies going back to high school. My mom tried to get me help by taking me to see them head doctors but that just let her know how fucked up I really was. They told her that I was having psychotic episodes and gave me a bunch of pills that didn't do shit but make me sleep. My father wasn't having it and threw them down the toilet and flushed them.

I started having the blackouts when I was 19 after my first body. It was some nigga that called himself trying to have my little brother jumped all because of some pussy. Last thing I remember is hitting him one time and I blacked out.

When I came to half his face was gone and my father and his cleaners were there.

After my first body I got this happy adrenaline rush that made me feel good. Killing was literally the only thing that could put a smile on my face. Not money, not sex, but watching death.

My parents each in their own way tried to help me. My mama tried but failed. My dad succeeded in helping me rain in my urges and focus them on being silent, meticulous, and deadly. He's the only one that can control me when I have my blackouts. He told me that he had the same mental issues growing up and that he was sorry his genes did me in. It's okay though because I have made plenty of money from my illness.

I had well over seven figures spread out all over Northern America,

Caribbean, and Switzerland. I have put in work for gangsters, politicians, governments, cartels, and regular people. I was just that damn good. The only thing I had yet to accomplish was finding the mutherfucker who was responsible for killing my Mama. She was my heart and any love I had in it died the day she was raped and murdered.

I have been searching for clues for the past two years and have turned up nothing. My dad hasn't been the same since he lost her. You would think that with the connections that we both have that we would have found something but we haven't found a damn clue. I know in my heart that whoever did it was a professional because they didn't leave one speck of evidence just my mama's beaten and bloody body.

Since her death my blackouts have gotten worse and I have nightmares about her. The phone rang and took me out of my thoughts. I looked at the screen and saw it was Raymond calling me.

"Where you at big bro?" he screamed in my ear.

"I'm at the condo what's up Ray? I said as I pulled on my Calvin Klein briefs.

"That bitch there with you?!" he said with a nasty tone.

I knew he was talking about this jump off I had named Tyesha. She was a bad chick that I fucked from time to time when I needed a release. She's about 5'5 and 120 pounds with a slim thick frame. She has her hair cut short in some sort of spiky hairstyle all the time. Dark chocolate complexion and she has honey colored eyes.

My brother and father couldn't stand her cause she got a mouth on her and is the definition of gold digger. We've been fucking for about a year but I don't do serious relationships so she is shit out of luck. Even if I ever did settle down she would be the last person I'd wife. I strap up with two condoms and I don't trust that! I make sure when I'm about to shoot my seeds I do so outside her body. I take the condoms and flush them myself. She's a true trap bitch and she will never make me her meal ticket.

"Naw man she ain't here. You on your way?"

"Yeah man I'm about to pick you up so we can go to the club to meet up with Ace. He's throwing a coming home and birthday party for his sister."

I scrunched my nose up.

"The only sister I know is Akia is and I know her damn birthday was last month."

Raymond started laughing.

"He has two sisters Ro. Akia is the youngest and apparently this other sister is a year older than her so she's 21. He said she's been away at school and finally coming home."

I heard a horn blowing outside. I peeped out and saw Raymond pulling in.

"Let me throw on some clothes and I'll be out in about 10.

I hung up, went to my closet, and threw on some True religion dark blue jeans, dark blue Polo shirt, and my dark blue custom Nikes. I don't do a lot of jewelry or grills. I had on my black and white Diamond Rolex and a 3 carat black diamond stud in my ear. I sprayed some Creed on and headed out the door. I hopped in my brothers Black Range Rover and shut the door.

"I ain't staying long Raymond I got shit to do. You know I don't do clubs."

"Man shut the fuck up you ain't got shit to do Ro but sit in the damn house. You can come out and show some love for Ace and his fam for a little while man."

I shook my head knowing I wasn't going to win this argument. I sat back not knowing that my life was about to change.

Chapter 3-Aja

I was standing in the mirror in the private bathroom in my brother's office at Club D-Nights. I was putting on my MAC lip gloss and wondering if the contents of my stomach would stay down. I had been through hell the past four years of my life and I wondered if I was making the right decision to come out of hiding.

I woke up four years ago in the hospital surrounded by my family. At first I was disoriented but then it all came back to me. My boyfriend that didn't give two fucks about me was beheaded in front of me and I was sexually assaulted and kidnapped by some sick ass stalker. After five days of being in the hospital and answering questions from multiple detectives, I was released.

I tried to get my life back to normal but he wouldn't let me. There were flowers showing up at my house or at school every day. I talked to my best friend Kyra and she had me move in with her and her mom to get away. It worked for a few months but then the flowers started coming with gifts this time. My brother Ace was running around trying to find out who he was but it just kept getting worse.

I moved to Memphis to go to college after homeschooling and receiving my high school diploma. I thought I would be safe after over 1 year of not hearing from my stalker. I was doing well in my freshman year and had a boyfriend named Tyler. He was so patient with me and allowed me to go at my own pace with our relationship. I even spent Christmas with him and his family. He gave me a beautiful ruby promise ring and said he loved me and would upgrade me to a diamond when we both graduated.

New Year's Eve night which was also my 18th birthday I decided to give him my virginity. I had decorated my dorm room with candles and flowers. My roommate was still away for the holidays as was most the students and I knew we would have our privacy. I was nervous as I put on the white see through thong set I bought from Victoria Secret. I took my hair out of its usual bun and let it flow down my back stopping at my bra line. I sprayed on some Daisy by Marc Jacobs and laid on the bed waiting for Tyler to come in. I waited for hours and called and texted him but he never answered.

I fell asleep waiting for him. I woke up feeling like my head was heavy. When I turned my head the clock read two pm. What the hell!! I tried to move but my head was banging and my body was sore. I looked down and realized I was naked and there was blood on my thighs. My vagina was sore as hell. I thought, *did Tyler come in last night and I don't remember?* But just then I saw the familiar bouquet of red and yellow roses and immediately felt sick to my stomach. It had a birthday card sitting in front of the vase. I slowly got up feeling dizzy and sick to my stomach and picked up the card. It read,

"*To my angel on her 18th birthday, I'm sorry I have been away from you but I told you I was always watching. You tried to give what was mine to that lame ass nigga. I'm not mad I know how innocent and trusting you are so I don't blame you my sweet. I told you I would claim you on your 18th and I had the best night of my life making love to you. I wanted to have your body all to myself so I put a little chloroform over your mouth so you wouldn't feel the pain of giving yourself to me. You taste just like the pineapples you love to eat and you kept yourself nice and tight for me. My dick was in heaven and your shit curved like it was made for me. I left some aspirin in case you have a headache and a nice hot Epsom salt bubble bath for the aches I left between your thighs. I also left the best gift of all,* *my seeds are in you so you can give me a baby. Don't try that Plan B shit or I will have to settle for 2nd best and go share my gift with Akia. P.S. Don't worry about that lame as nigga either. People that fuck with mine get fucked."* Love always your eternity. "*

I broke down in the middle of the floor and started hysterically crying. My stomach churned and I ran to the bathroom and threw up everything in my stomach until I was dry heaving. I got in the shower and scrubbed until I turned red. Hoping and praying that I didn't get pregnant by his sick ass. I got out and called Ace and told him what happened. He was going crazy telling me to stay put and he was on the way. I couldn't believe that he has taken two more things from me, Tyler and my virginity.

Two weeks later they found Tyler floating in a lake with his penis cut off and shoved up his ass. I cried for months after that and went into a self-imposed exile. I moved to Gatlinburg in a cabin my brother paid for with cash and put in someone else's name. He gave me a fake ID with another name and twenty thousand in cash to live off of. Kyra decided she would come and live with me so I wouldn't be in the mountains alone. I signed up for online classes so I could finish my degree.

Six weeks later I found out I was indeed pregnant. After hearing the news I was devastated but I didn't believe in abortions so I knew I would give this baby up for adoption. It was not needed. I miscarried four weeks later. I was sad but thanked God that I didn't have to carry that monsters child anymore. I didn't leave the cabin unless it was to go to the store or doctor's office for the next two and a half years. Kyra was my saving grace and kept me sane. I didn't visit my family and told them not to come to see me. I didn't trust that he wouldn't find me by following them.

Kyra and I used cash for everything never leaving a paper trail. On Christmas day a few weeks ago I got a call on my burner phone from Mama telling me that she wanted me to come home because she was sick. I thought about it and knew it was time for me to come home. I couldn't hide forever.

So here I stand in my brother's office bathroom ready to see my family I haven't seen in over two years and also to face the demon that awaited me. I heard the bathroom door opened and Kyra came in.

"Girl what is taking you so long? You always are going to be pretty as hell so you can stop trying!" She said with her hand on her thick thighs.

I looked at my best friend and she was killing the game tonight in a black leather cat suit with a plunging neckline and some black red bottoms on her feet. She's about 5'3 and curvy like me with a dark chocolate complexion and gray eyes. She has shoulder length naturally curly hair all around her face and she had it pinned to one side tonight.

"I'm coming Ky I just needed a minute. You know I haven't been around a lot of people in a long time. I can't wait to see Akia and Ace, I miss them so much." I said with a sigh.

I turned around and smoothed out the black off the shoulder shirt and black leather high waist shorts Ky bought for me to wear. They had all my thick ass thighs out shaking my head. She had paired the outfit with some gladiator gold high heel sandals. I had on Gold hoops and my hair was straightened down my back with thin gold bands at the front. I had an arm full of gold bracelets to help set it off. I knew we both were looking good tonight and I needed the extra courage to face my family and my demons.

Tyesha

"He bet not have his ass in some bitch's face when I get here!" I said to my girl Camille.

Let me introduce myself. My name is Tyesha Simone Sims and I am that bitch! Hate all you want but I am fine as hell and get what I want. I am 5'5 with short spiky hair and a chocolate goddess! They go crazy for my honey eyes and slim body with apple booty. My main love was money!! I get it whenever and however I like!

I grew up living with my daddy and Uncle because my mama died right after having me. My daddy was a pimp and so was my Uncle Damon. I have a half-sister named Kyra but I couldn't stand that bitch! She thought she was better than everybody.

Tonight I was on my way to the club to see my man Ro. This nigga is fine as hell and has long paper. I've been trying to trap his ass with a baby for a year and he won't cooperate. What?!

Yes, call me a gold digger because this bitch shovels for gold honey. His brother and daddy couldn't stand my ass but oh well they better get used to me being in the family.

"I don't know why you keep going after this man he don't want nothing from you but what's between your legs!" Camille laughed.

"Oh you mean like how Ace does you? At least Ro will take me out in public!" I said rolling my eyes at her stupid ass.

Camille was dumb as hell; literally. The only reason I kept her around is she would do whatever I want. She's a gorgeous girl with gray eyes and an almost white complexion. She's mixed with because her mama is Italian and her daddy is black. Her daddy is Big C, a retired kingpin so her ass is spoiled and rich.

"You know Ace can't claim me right now. He is trying to find the right time to tell daddy about us." she said in that whiny ass voice.

Truth be told Ace could care less about her ass. He was just stringing her along. We pulled up to the valet in front of the club and I stepped out of my black BMW like the bad bitch I was. I was rocking a Dolce and Gabbana white midi dress that stopped right under my ass and my girls up top were on full display. I was rocking my red Manolo's on my freshly pink pedicured toes. All eyes were on us. I strutted to the VIP entrance and was waved through by security. They knew who I was since I had been here several times with Ro.

We walked through the club like we owned it. All type of ballers was trying to get my attention but I was only looking for one. We got to Ace's section and saw Ace, Raymond, and Ro were lounging on the gold and white sectional tossing back Hennessey. I pulled my dress down and strolled over with an extra sway in my hips to my man. Raymond was the first to look up.

"Well if it isn't Thotesha and Dumbmille! I see hoes still travel in packs!!! He said loudly!!

Ace and Raymond fell on the floor laughing while Ro had that weird as smirk on his face.

"Fuck you Ray! You ain't shit!" I screamed with my hands on my hips.

"Ro you ain't going to say nothing to your brother?" Camille asked.

"For what? She is a thot and you dumb as hell." He said looking nonchalant.

"So I'm a thot now! You wasn't saying that when I was sucking your dick last night! Why you still deal with me if I'm a thot Ro!!" I said getting in his face.

He stood up and towered over me and I immediately started thinking I went too far by getting in his face. He stared down at me with an evil look on his face. Raymond and Ace got up and slowly approached him.

"Ro man this bitch ain't worth it. Just calm down and let's go down to the bar and get another drink." Ace said in a low and calm voice.

Ro backed away from me but still had those evil ass eyes on me. He finally turned and started to walk away but stopped at the entrance of VIP and spoke with Ace's bodyguard Tan.

"Get that bitch out of our VIP section and don't let her back in."

He walked off towards the bar and I was finally able to release the breath I was holding.

Tan walked over to me and said "Tyesha you gotta go Ma. You heard boss man."

I looked at Camille and told her let's go. As we were headed out of VIP two leather clad figures were walking in. The closer they got the more pissed off I grew. Where did these bitches come from? I haven't seen them since high school. I looked at my sister Kyra and her friend Aja.

My sister Kyra still looked beautiful with those damn gray eyes she got from her mama. I hated being around her because she always stole the show. Then I peeped out Aja. She had gotten thicker in all the right places and her hair had grown down her back. She was even prettier than she was in high school. Oh hell naw I wasn't leaving anywhere. Ro might want one of them and that was a no go in my eyes. I stomped over to my so called sister.

"Well look who decided to come out of hiding. Kyra you can't speak to your only sister?" I said throwing shade at Aja since they called each other sisters.

"Tyesha you know we don't get along and you know why! If you don't want people knowing your secrets you will leave me the hell alone." Kyra said trying to pass by me.

I put my hand on her arm stopping her.

"Bitch you don't want your secrets out either so I suggest you watch who the fuck you're talking too!" I made sure I dug my nails into her arm to back up my point.

"Get your nasty ass hands off of her, Tyesha!" Aja screamed and this bitch pushed me down!

Camille's scary ass took off running towards security. I got up and was about to tear her ass up when Ace, Raymond, and Ro came running over to VIP.

"Tyesha I know you weren't about to put your damn hands on my sister!! Ace shouted getting in my face.

"Ace she ain't stupid!! She can get froggy if she want!!" Aja screamed trying to get around Ace. Just when I was about to get in her ass gunshots rang out.

POP! POP! POP!

Everybody started running and ducking for cover. Just my damn luck!!!!!

Chapter 4-Ro

We were chilling at the bar when Tan came over and told us Tyesha was about to get into a fight over there in VIP. Her ass was getting on my nerves with her ratchet ass attitude.

Ace looked over towards VIP and jumped up damn near running people over and shouted, "Man that's my sister she's about to fight!"

I followed him over to VIP and my heart damn near stopped once I peeped the shorty talking crazy to Tyesha. She was milk chocolate and thick as hell in them leather shorts. But what had me gone is how beautiful her face was especially her eyes. Every time her neck rolled her hair would fall in her face. I had the urge to reach and run my fingers through it.

I was snapped out of my thoughts as gunshots rang out. I immediately grabbed my two nines out and started shooting in the direction of the shots being fired towards VIP.

"Ro get my sister!!!" Ace yelled while firing back behind the couch.

I peeped shorty hiding behind one of the chairs and grabbed her still firing back at whoever was shooting at us. Ace had a hidden door behind the couch so I dragged her with me behind the couch and shoved her through the hidden door.

"Ace and Ray come on!!" I said firing back in the direction of the shots.

They ducked down and went through the door with the shorty that was with his sister. I looked around to see if I could see who was firing but I couldn't see shit. I ducked down and went through the door that led to Ace's office through a hidden wall. When I came out into Ace's office he had one arm around his sister and he was on the phone with the other.

"Akia don't come to the club! Scoop up April and head to the safe house! He screamed hanging up the phone.

"Ace why is it that every time I come out of hiding I end up getting people hurt!! Aja screamed as tears were running down her face.

I had an unexpected urge to wipe those tears away and keep her safe.

"Man that shit was crazy! Ro man did you see who was firing at us? "Ray said as he paced the floor mad.

"Naw man it was too damn dark in there. All I know is I will find out and it won't be pretty." I said shaking my head.

I felt eyes on me and looked up to see Aja looking at me with a smile on her face. She still had tears falling but that smile had me feeling some type of way.

Usually when I went into beast mode people would turn their head or run. Not baby girl, she looked at me straight in my eyes.

"Aja are you alright? Her friend asked while rubbing Aja's back.

"Yes, Kyra I will be alright. You know me. It just threw me off. Just know your sister will see me real soon." she said rolling her eyes.

So her friend was Tyesha's sister. Damn, small world. Now that I looked at her I saw the resemblance. The dark chocolate smooth skin and the same shape but Tyesha was smaller. Only other differences between them were she had gray eyes and was much prettier than Tyesha. She also seemed to have a better attitude.

"Ace do you think it was him?" Aja asked looking up at her brother with fear in her eyes.

"Naw sis, I think this was about me. Nobody knew you were here except my boys, April, and

Kia. You good here Aja, don't worry." Ace said reassuring his sister.

"Who the fuck is him, Ace?" Raymond asked when I was about to ask the same thing.

Ace looked at Aja for confirmation on if it was okay to tell them. She looked hesitant but Ace assured her we were cool. Ace told us about this sick ass mutherfucker who had been stalking her since she was sixteen. He told us about him killing her boyfriends and raping her. When Ace got to the rape part I saw Aja cringe and tears start to come down her face. I walked over to her not even realizing I was touching her face until she looked up.

"Baby girl as long as I have breath in my body he won't touch you ever again." I said in my calm but deadly voice to let her know I was serious.

We stared at each other until my rude ass brother interrupted.

"Aww hell naw Beast done met his beauty!!!
He said cracking up on the floor.

"Hell no Ro that's my sister you staring at!
She is off limits to your crazy ass!!! What's up
with you Aja you always attracting the crazy
ones!" Ace said making his sister laugh.

"No but on a serious tip I need to hit the
streets to find out who was crazy enough to be
shooting at us. Ro can you take Aja and Kyra to
your crib? I don't trust leaving the ladies by
themselves." Ace said while gathering his keys.

"Yeah I'll take them to my house not the
condo." Ray and Ace looked at me strange
because they knew I never took anyone there. I
don't trust mutherfuckers to know where I lay my
head. Ace, Ray, Akia, and my Pops were the only
ones who knew where I lived. I took everybody
else to my condo especially Tyesha. She was
shady as fuck and I didn't trust that she wouldn't
set my ass up.

"Come on ladies Tan just texted and said its all clear to come out." Ace said as he placed his nine in his back.

"The ladies followed Ace and Ray out the door and I followed behind them to cover their backs. I was always aware of my surroundings. It was one of the things that Pops taught us. Being a hit man just enhanced that trait.

I also couldn't help looking at the nice view of Aja in them leather shorts looking good as hell. My second head was starting to pay too much attention so I looked elsewhere. When we got to the back parking area, Tan was there with his Sig pulled looking around. I trained him well.

Tan was Cuban and had curly hair and stood around 6'1 at about 180 pounds. We called him Tan because he loved going to the pool to get tans. He was a pretty boy but deadly. I trained him and placed him as Ace's bodyguard three years ago. He used to be a hit man like me but his ex-wife had a baby girl and he didn't want to go for runs out of town.

We walked over to Ace's Porsche Cayenne and he and Raymond opened their doors.

"Here are my keys bro don't wreck my shit trying to side eye shorty." Ray said as he tossed me the keys.

"Fuck you Ray gon somewhere." I said as I walked over to his Range

Rover.

I unlocked the doors and held the door open to the backseat for both ladies to climb in. I didn't want them upfront in case anything went down.

"Buckle up ladies. I got ya." I said and started the car and pulled into traffic. Little did I know we were being watched by several pairs of eyes.

Chapter 5- "Unknown"

My heart almost stopped when I heard she was back in town. I have been looking for my angel everywhere. I wonder if she had my son or daughter. I hope it was a girl so I could treat her like a princess.

I had to go to the club to see her and also to make sure she doesn't get away from me again. She turns twenty one tomorrow and I know it's time to make my move. As soon as I got in the club I see her in VIP. She is even more gorgeous than she was the last time I saw her. She now has the look of a woman and not little girl. She is my future and I have to have her.

I was about to move closer when gunshots rang out. I ducked down and started looking for my angel but when I looked at VIP it was empty. Where the fuck did she go?! I started to panic but then I remembered there was a back entrance to the club and I know Ace would get his sister out of harm's way. I took my place in the shadows and wait. I release the breath I was holding when I saw Ace, Ro, Raymond, Kyra, and my angel walk out.

I thought she would leave with Ace but she got in the car with Ro. "Fuck!!" I said hitting the steering wheel hard. With Ro around getting to my angel would be harder. But never impossible for me. If Ro got in the way he would get dealt with like the rest.

Tyesha

I watched as these two bitches got in the car with my man. His ass didn't even come to check and see if I was dead or not!!! I don't know where the hell Camille is with her scary ass.

I was waiting on my ride to scoop me up. As soon as I was about to text him again he pulled up in his custom F150 truck. I climbed in to greet my man. Yes, nosy asses I said my man! He was the father of my four year old twins Dajae and Daria. We have known each other all of our lives but being together in public was a no go. I will explain that later. Ro had no clue I had kids or was seeing somebody else. I have love for Ro but he is just a means to an end and that end was money.

"Hey baby I thought I told you to wait until I gave you the signal to shoot Ace?!" I said while closing the door and putting on my seatbelt.

"I couldn't help it, Tyesha. I have been waiting to kill that mutherfucker for four years!!! I know he killed my brother! I would have been got him if I didn't get locked up after the funeral. Desmond and I had the plan all together to get Ace and Big C. I don't know what happened to fuck it up but I will find out!!" He said as he took a hit off his blunt.

I shook my head because I knew it was no reasoning with him when it came to avenging the death of his twin brother Desmond. I was still hurt to this day by his death. I loved Desmond and we were going to be a family until he was murdered. Yes, I know call me trifling for fucking two brothers. Judge all you want but I loved both of them. They knew I was with them both so it wasn't any sneaking around. We all lived together and had plans set in place so we wouldn't have to worry about money for the rest of our lives.

Desmond was going to get close to Aja and Ace and kill them both but something happened and Desmond ended up chopped up in a van. Derrick got caught with some drugs and ended up serving four years after the funeral so we had to come up with a new plan.

I was to get close to Ro and get inside information on the D-City Boyz.

Derrick was going to lay low and kill them off one by one until he could take over as King of the city. No one knew Desmond had a twin or that I was his cousin.

What?! Yes, Desmond and Derrick are my first cousins. Uncle Damon raised us to keep it in the family. Derrick is the one who took my virginity when I was 14.

My Daddy and Uncle said it was time for me to start learning how to use my talents as a woman to help the family come up. Back in the day cousins married cousins all the time. Yes, I married Derrick while he was in jail. So he was my husband and I was going to make sure that he got everything he deserved. If that meant killing all the D-City Boyz then so be it. We pulled up to our apartment and got out walking up the stairs and into the living room.

"Where are the girls Babe?" I said taking off my heels.

"Daddy took them tonight so I can get my dick wet. It's been four years since I had some of my pussy. Take them clothes off and welcome your man home." He said as he pulled out his eight inches and started stroking his mans.

I got down on my knees and put him in my mouth and started welcoming my husband home.

Ace

I couldn't believe someone tried to take me out in my own damn club. D-City Nights was my baby and I had put a lot of blood, sweat, and tears into making it the hottest club in the city. Luckily, I had insurance and it could be repaired. But, the look of fear on my sister's face is what had me heated.

I have been the protector of the family since I was a youngster thanks to my no good ass Mama April. She drank up all the money she got from public assistance and child support. We would go hungry for days sometimes or be without lights for days until I went out and stole or hustled to keep us afloat. I called her April because she was never a mother to any of us. I made sure my sisters went to school and got an education so they wouldn't have to go without if I wasn't around. I lucked out and hooked up with Big C and started making paper.

After he stepped down I took over and grew the empire along with Ro and Ray.

Thinking back on the night I couldn't get Kyra off my mind. What nobody knew is that Kyra and I used to mess around before all the shit went down with Aja. She was my heart and one day she told me that we couldn't see each other anymore. I was devastated and couldn't believe that she dropped me without a real explanation. Seeing her pretty ass tonight had those old feelings that never left coming back. I never have loved anyone but her.

I was messing around with Big C's daughter Camille but she was just something to pass the time. Don't get me wrong Camille was a nice girl but she didn't have any ambition for anything but to be a kingpin's wife. I wanted someone who was a boss like me. I don't mind spoiling someone that's on my level. I know I was fucking up by messing with Camille but I couldn't help myself. I was lonely and she filled a corner of the void that Kyra left.

My phone rang pulling me out of my thoughts.

"Ace Mama said how long are we supposed to stay here? She said she has a date." My sister Akia said sounded irritated.

I laughed because I knew April was getting on her nerves.

"Akia tell April at least until tomorrow. She gonna have to stay in tonight."

Raymond's eyes shot up when I said Akia's name.

"Is that my wifey on the phone?" He started trying to grab my phone.

"Move your thirsty ass away from me Ray!! You just saw her ass this morning." I said putting the phone up to my ear away from him.

Akia and Raymond were engaged and getting married in a few months. I was mad at first when they started talking because I felt she was too young but, I got used to it and was happy she had a good man.

"You an old hating ass dread-headed mutherfucker for keeping me away from my wifey! He said looking like a lost puppy in the passenger seat.

I shook my head, "Akia get your man before I beat his ass. Here talk to him." I threw the phone and hit him in the chest with it.

"Hey wifey what's up?" They started chit chatting and I zoned the lovey dovey crap out.

I needed to focus and figure out who was trying to kill us. I needed to clear my head and stop thinking about Kyra and start figuring out who was after me. I also needed to protect Aja from her crazy ass stalker. It looked like I might have help with that situation the way Ro was eyeing Aja down. The way things were going I would need all the help I could get.

Chapter 6-Kyra

I cannot believe all the shit that went down tonight. I looked over at Aja and she had nodded off against the window. I am so glad my girl is getting some rest because she has been through hell these past couple of years. Aja was like my sister more than my friend and I would do anything to protect her.

My sister Tyesha was my flesh and blood but she was a snake. I learned that the hard way and it cost me the man that I have loved since I was in middle school. When I saw Ace tonight my heart literally was beating out of my chest when he ran up in VIP.

When the gunshots went off he grabbed me and pushed me behind the couch. He fell on top of me and for a brief moment we stared at each other like we used to. Once we were all safe I couldn't help but to see how fine he has become.

His dreads were longer now going to the middle of his back but he still kept them tipped at the ends in red. His muscles were bulging through his Polo shirt he had on with his True religion jeans and he had grown man swag about him now. I felt his eyes studying me as well and felt chills run down my spine every time he looked my way. I knew I would be changing my underwear if he kept licking his lips. It was a habit he always did when he was in deep thought. I wished I could run and tell him how much I loved him but that could never happen. Too many secrets were in my past and if he ever found them out, he would kill me literally. Ace was a hothead and didn't trust too many people. That's how he got the scar that ran down the side of his face. Trying to protect his Mama April from getting beat up by her then boyfriend Monty. He saw Monty hit April and proceeded to beat his ass. April was mad at Ace for beating up her man and sliced him with a knife so he would stop.

From that day forward I watched his heart get colder unless it had to do with Aja and Akia. We started messing around in my junior year of high school.

We decided to keep it a secret because he was deep in the middle of a war between Big C and someone named D-Money. He didn't want me to become collateral damage if they started going after loved ones.

We dated secretly until I broke up with him right after Aja left my house for college. He was devastated and so was I but I had to. If I stayed with him my past would come back to haunt us both. I couldn't have that. I had to protect my secret by giving up my heart. I jumped at the chance when Aja went into hiding so I could run too.

I got my phone out and text the one person that knew everything. My mama and I moved out of town shortly after I broke up with Ace. We moved to Pegram in the country and laid low so they couldn't find us. I texted her and asked was everything okay and let her know what happened at the club. She said everything was good and make sure I stayed safe and watched my back. I told her I loved her and would be there this weekend to visit. I visited her every other week to ensure everything was alright. I looked out the window and saw that Ro was pulling up to White Castle.

"Hey ladies I'm going to get us something to eat because I don't have anything at the house. I am going to lock you in. My brother's car is bulletproof so nothing will get in. What you want to eat? Do you know what baby girl likes to eat?" He asked as he saw that Aja was asleep.

"Yes she likes their ranch chicken rings and cheeseburgers with extra pickle and ketchup, fries, and a root beer. I'll take the four cheeseburgers with no onions and a large cola."

He took his guns out of the glove compartment and put one in his back. The other he handed to me.

"Do you know how to use a gun?" He asked.

"Yes, Ace taught me and Aja how to shoot. He makes us go to the range every week. He also had us take self-defense classes. He wanted us to know how to protect ourselves after everything Aja went through."

He looked over at Aja and brushed the hair out of her face that had fallen while she slept. He pulled back when he noticed me looking and hurried out of the truck and locked us in. I looked over at Aja still sleeping and then looked at Ro walking into the building but looking everywhere at once to make sure his surroundings were straight. Yes, he is exactly what Aja needs.

Aja

I had fallen asleep in the car and woke up as soon as Ro got in the car with some food. We drove for another fifteen minutes pulling into the Belle Meade area with a lot of mini mansions and big mansions. Ro pulled into a long driveway that lead up a hill and at the top was a beautiful gray stucco home. I could tell it cost some money and had a lot of rooms. In the front it had a fountain and a large fence around the property. I also saw cameras everywhere.

Ro came around and opened the door for us and took my hand so he could help me out. As soon as our hands touched I felt a spark and shivered. This man was too damn fine. We started to walk up the steps and I realized he still had my hand in his. He let go to push in a code and his fingerprint on a state of the art security panel. I immediately felt safer with all this security around which is something I hardly ever felt.

He opened the door and the whole downstairs was open. There was a sunken living room, kitchen, and dining room. They were huge and the kitchen looked like something out of a magazine. The colors for each room were done in black and gold. The floors were a black hardwood with white area rugs in the living room.

"Aja and Kyra y'all can go in the kitchen at the island and start eating. I need to get your rooms ready and make some calls." he said as he took the black and gold marble stairs that I'm sure lead to more luxury.

We started dividing up the food and I placed Ro's in the microwave so it would stay warm. We sat at the island and could see a huge pool out of the sliding doors.

"Girl this man is paid and fine! You lucked out little sis." Kyra said while sipping on her drink.

"He is not my man girl, shut up! He is fine as hell though but I am not going there. You know I can't risk being with anyone while he is out there." I said in between chewing on my chicken ring.

"Aja you know I love you but you can't be scared to live your life because of his sick ass! That man upstairs looks like he can take care of you and himself. I don't think he scares too easily." She said shaking her head.

I was just about to comment when Ro came downstairs.

"Aja can I talk to you for a minute?" Ro said in that deep voice that made me weak.

"Sure it's fine."

He opened up the sliding doors and walked out to the pool deck and sat down on a chaise lounge and I sat down on the one beside him.

"I need you to tell me everything you can remember about the guy that's after you. Any detail that you can remember." Ro said as he stared at me with those light brown eyes.

"I don't remember much because the first time he wore a mask and the second time I was drugged when he raped me. I do remember his voice which was very deep and he wore cologne I will never forget the scent of. I also remember the room he kept me in. It was white with a large black canopy bed in the middle with white satin sheets. He called it my princess room. It had pictures of me all over the walls from when I was a little girl until I was sixteen. It was creepy as hell." I started shaking just thinking about his crazy ass. Ro must have noticed and pulled me from the chaise lounge into his lap.

"Baby girl I'm sorry you went through that shit but you don't have to worry about him anymore. I got you and I will die before I let him touch you." He said with a determined look.

I placed my head on his shoulder and closed my eyes.

"That's the thing Ro I don't want you to die for me. Every man that has gotten close to me he has killed. I know I've only known you a short time but I already care about you and don't want you to die because of me."

He pulled my head off of his shoulder and placed both of his large hands on each side of my head and looked into my eyes.

"Aja I am hard to kill, and no man puts fear in my heart. If I say I got you than you damn sure better believe me baby girl." He leaned in and kissed me softly on my lips.

We started kissing and I was melting in his arms. I moaned as he deepened the kiss and laid me down on the chaise lounge. I was scared of my reaction as he moved his hands up my thighs where the shorts had rode up. But instead of fear I felt tingles shooting through my body. He sat up and pulled his shirt off and pulled down my shorts taking them off exposing my lace thong.

He started rubbing his fingers up and down my slit gathering the juices that were leaking through and placed them in his mouth sucking the juices. He looked at me and said, "Are you sure you want this baby girl? I know you haven't been with anyone and I can wait..." I interrupted him by taking off my thong, shirt, and bra.

I laid back on the chaise lounge and opened my legs to him. He immediately dove in head first and started sucking and licking everywhere. The pleasure he was creating had me seeing black spots behind my eyes. The pressure was building and I couldn't help screaming his name.

"Ro I'm about to cum!"

"Give that shit up to me baby girl!"

As soon as he said that I was erupting in his mouth and he continued to lick and suck sending aftershocks all through my body. After begging for mercy he stood up and took off his pants and briefs. His manhood stood at full attention and I began to get nervous. He looked every bit of ten inches and it was thick with a curve to it. He must have seen my fear and he started covering me in kisses from the top of my head to my toes.

He came back up and started licking and sucking on my nipples which caused me to get wet as hell. He used his fingers to get me wetter and when I felt like I was about to burst again and couldn't take anymore. I knew I was ready to give him all of me. "Ro I'm ready.

Ro

I looked down at this beautiful woman that has been through hell and she is so strong for her age.

"Are you sure baby girl?"

She shook her head yes and I eased into her slowly because she was tight as hell. Plus, I know her only experience with sex had been the rape and I planned on making those memories of sex fade away. I wanted her to think about me when she thought about making love.

I kept easing in and sucking on her neck and breast until I was fully in. I had to stop for a minute to keep from busting. She had the best cat I ever had. It was tight and warm and gripping the shit out of my mans.

I started moving again and when she started moaning and opening her legs more I started going in on her hitting that sweet spot. I felt her cat tightening and getting wetter and I knew she was about to cum again.

"Baby girl you gripping the fuck out my dick! Go on and let that shit go ma! I said moving faster and deeper.

Just as she called my name I couldn't hold it anymore and let go of all my kids in her. I felt dizzy by the time I was finished and we laid there in the chaise lounge sweating and breathing hard. I moved out of her and pulled her into my side. I looked down and she had immediately fallen asleep. I brushed the hair off of her face and looked at how innocent she looked while she slept.

I don't know how the fuck this happened so fast but I was really feeling her.

I thought about how we only met a few hours ago but here I was a few minutes ago making love to her. I wasn't in love I don't think because I never felt that before. But, I know I care about her more than I have ever cared about anyone. I would die to protect her. Ace and I were going to have to have a serious talk about baby girl because she wasn't going anywhere but my bed.

I could protect her here better than he could because he was the face of the D-City Boyz and needed to be in the streets. I always disappeared for jobs and stayed in the shadows. I just prayed that I could handle the emotions that Aja was stirring up in me. I was afraid to go to sleep for fear she would be the victim of one of my nightmares or witness one of my blackouts.

I eased away from Aja and put my clothes back on. I took my T-shirt I had on up under my shirt and gently placed it over her body. I picked her up in my arms bridal style and carried her through the kitchen and upstairs. I took her to the room beside mine and placed her gently under the covers and kissed her lips.

I closed the door behind me and ran into Kyra walking down the hallway.

"Aja asleep?" she asked.

"Yeah baby girl is sleeping. Your room okay?" I said walking towards my door.

"It's more than fine. Thanks for letting us stay here Ro. My girl needs protecting. She is strong but fragile at the same time. Be patient with her because she's afraid to let anybody get too close to her. You are the first person I've seen that she has trusted in a while so don't fuck up or you will have to deal with me!"

She said trying to be hard.

I respected her because she was looking out for her friend and Aja needed loyalty.

"I got you little bit. I won't hurt her or let her be hurt by anybody."

She nodded and started down the hall to her room. I was opening the door when she stopped me with the next set of words that came out of her mouth.

"Ro speaking of protection I sure hope you used some because if you fucking around with my nasty ass sister Tyesha and gave Aja something I will kill you. Goodnight bro!" she said chuckling as she closed the door.

I opened my bedroom door shaking my head because I knew I was clean because I got tested every month. Plus I never went in raw with Tyesha or any woman. I strapped up twice with her because I knew she was shady. I took a shower and was about to doze off when it came to me.

"Oh shit I didn't strap up this time I hit Aja raw!" She really got my mind gone. I didn't even think twice about it and I dropped seeds all off in her. Ace is going to kill me if my Pops didn't first. That was my last thought before drifting off to sleep.

Chapter 7-Aja

I woke up feeling disoriented and wondering where I was when I remembered I was safe in Ro's house. I looked over and didn't see him in the bed beside me and wondered where he was. I looked at the clock and it said ten in the morning. I never sleep this late. I guess it was the workout that Ro gave me last night.

I can't believe I gave it up on the first night. I thought shaking my head. I hope he doesn't think I'm a hoe. Last night was everything and I hoped it wouldn't be the last time. I got up and went to the bathroom and took care of my hygiene.

When I came back out I noticed that on the dresser was a white Chanel maxi dress and white and gold Chanel heels to match. There was also a bag from

Victoria Secret with a bra and panty set. As I was about to take off the robe I had on Kyra came in the door looking pretty in a black PINK sweat suit.

"Girl that man must have put it on you last night. I had to go to the mall by myself and get us something to wear." She said laughing as she sat down on the bed.

"Kyra you so damn nosy. How much do I owe you for the clothes? And where is Ro?" I said trying to avoid the topic of my night with Ro.

"You don't owe me any money. Your man gave me his black card and told me to get his baby girl anything she needed. He said he had to go meet up with the boys and his dad for breakfast. He also told me to tell you he will pick you up for lunch." Kyra said with a smug look on her face.

I couldn't stop the smile that spread across my face. Ro was so sweet under that hard exterior.

"Well thanks for picking me out something nice to wear. I guess I will figure out a way today for us to go and pick-up our things." I said while brushing my hair and putting it into a high ponytail.

"Girl your man told me to fill up the closet for you." she said and openedthe walk in closet door.

It was filled to capacity with all kinds of clothes, shoes, and bags.

"Kyra you spent too much! Ro is going to kill us!" I yelled because I didn't want him to think I was after him for his money.

"Ro is who told me to fill up both our closets or he would be offended and do it himself. Aja calm down and let that man take care of you." She said as she walked towards the door.

"I'm sorry Ky I'm really trying to be normal but it's so hard after years of being paranoid. I just don't want to wear out my welcome with Ro." I said after taking a deep breath and calming down.

"Girl after what you two were doing on the patio last night I wouldn't worry about wearing out your welcome. I would worry about him wearing out something else!" she laughed as she opened the door.

"Kyra please tell me you didn't hear us last night. "I said turning red.

"Y'all nasty asses forgot I was in the kitchen eating. I almost threw up my food!" I had to go upstairs and finish my food. You know I've been dick deprived! I had to go and take a cold shower after listening to the both of y'all! Don't be embarrassed you needed that Aja. Now get dressed so we can watch a movie before Ro comes and scoops you up. He got a movie theatre in the basement. I picked us up some Waffle House to eat while we watch." She said heading out the door.

I shook my head at my crazy outspoken best friend and finished putting on the dress and sandals. I smoothed down my edges and made sure my ponytail was straight. I looked good and I couldn't wait for my lunch date with Ro. I was still nervous about getting with him because of my track record. My stalker could take him away from me and I know my heart couldn't take it. I just prayed that everything would be alright and that I would finally catch a break.

Rodney

I was finishing up scrambling the eggs and putting cheese in them while the bacon was cooking in the oven. My boys would be here soon and eat me out of a house and home. This was our thing ever since the love of my life and their mama

Evette was murdered. I loved both my boys so much and they were the only thing I had left of her.

Raymond my youngest was just like her laid back and always making us laugh. Ro was all me bad temper and all. He hasn't been the same since Evette died. I heard the alarm for the door go off and I knew it was one of my sons. Ro and Ray came in the same time talking low.

"Morning boys the foods almost ready. Where's Ace?" I said looking out the window to see if I saw his car.

"He should be here any minute Pops he had to make a drop off on the way." Ray said as he stuffed a blueberry muffin in his mouth.

That boy was slim but can eat more than anyone in the house. Ace was like a son to me so he was always included in our father and son Sunday breakfasts. I looked up at Ro and he wasn't saying much and looked to be in deep thought.

"Ro what's on your mind this morning son?" I said taking the bacon out of the oven.

"He's thinking about your daughter in law Pops." Ray laughed.

"Hell naw Ro tell me you ain't trying to wife that hoe!" I scrunched up my face because I know he ain't that crazy.

I have told him many times to get rid of Tyesha's ass but she seems to hang around like a bad disease.

"Pops come on now you know me better than that. She is not wifey material." Ro said reassuring me he hadn't completely lost his sense.

"Then who is Ray talking about?"

"He's talking about a shorty I met at the club last night before the shooting." Ro said.

"Speaking of the shooting did Ace figure out who was shooting at y'all?

"No sir he's still trying to figure it out. He supposed to be dropping off some money to someone that has some information." Ro said helping me place the food and juice on the table.

About that time I heard the door chime and Ace was walking in.

"What's up Pops? It smells good as hell in here. He said as he sat at the table.

We all started loading up our plates and sat around the table. I looked at my boys talking and joking with each other. I was so proud of the young men they had become. I had something important to tell them today and I hoped they would understand and not trip out.

"Hey boys I have to talk to you three about something important." I said as I wiped my mouth with a paper towel.

"What's up Pops you not dying are you?" Ray asked.

"Naw baby boy its nothing like that. You know how much I loved your moms and I would never disrespect her memory in anyway. Look I won't beat around the bush. I wanted to tell you all that I got a lady." I looked around the table to see their reactions.

Ace had a look like he knew something, Ray had a smirk on his face, and

Ro's face was blank which scared me.

"Pops I know who she is and I'm okay with you dating April. I saw her getting out of your Bentley last week. As long as you treat her right

I'm good with it." Ace said and shoved another piece of bacon in his mouth.

"Pops you dating April's scheming ass? No offense Ace but you know how your mama is. She'd sell her brain for a gallon of gin." Ray said looking concerned.

"No offense taken bro I know how she is. Pops watch yourself with her cause she ain't shit!" Ace said shaking his head.

"Ro why you so quiet, son?" I asked.

"I don't have anything to say about it. Do what you do." He stared at his plate.

"Son say what's on your mind don't shut down. I know how you feel about your mother and she will always be my first love. Just because I'm moving on doesn't mean I will forget her." I said trying to get him to talk to me.

I was glad Ace was on board because I was going to be in the family. Ray seemed okay with it but Ro was not going to be happy about me being with someone else. He was going to have to realize that I was in love and was tired of being lonely.

"Ace, I need to talk to you about Aja when you get a chance man." Ro said looking at Ace and ignoring me.

"She okay Ro? I know last night might have brought up some things for her." Ace said with a concerned look on his face.

"She's good man I got her. Just know she will be staying with me at the house." Ro said in a stern voice.

I spit out my coffee. "Ro what are you doing with Ace's sister at your house? You never let anybody but us know where you stay. Why is she staying with you? I asked confused on what the hell was going on and why nobody had told me about it."

"Pops my sister Aja is being stalked by some crazy ass mutherfucker that won't leave her alone. Since we were not sure on who was shooting at us I sent her with Ro for protection. Ro, what I want to know is what you got going on with my sister because you seem to be claiming something that doesn't belong to you." Ace said with a mean mug on his face.

Ace then went on to explain to me everything his sister had been through.

"Ace you know you my brother but you got too much going on right now to protect her full time. We don't know who is after her or us. Do you really think you can be there twenty four seven and keep her and Kyra safe? I have top level security at my house and I dare a mutherfucker to try me! They will have to kill me to get to her!" Ro yelled.

I didn't like this at all Ro never raised his voice especially at his best friend that he calls a brother.

"Ro I'm not sure you should be getting involved in this. You got a lot of shit yourself going on with the missions and now you want to add in being a bodyguard with a psycho mutherfucker that is known for killing people that get near her? Naw, son you don't want to get in the middle of that shit no offense Ace. Why don't you let me put someone on her and that way you know she's in good hands? I don't have a good feeling about you getting into this." I said with determination in my voice.

"Pops I love you but I know what I'm doing. Aja stays with me and that's that. Ace and Ray follow me to my house so we can come up with a game plan for both situations bye Pops I'll talk to you later." He said as he got up from the table and headed towards the door.

"Ray you better get your brother I don't play about Aja. Bye Pops!" Ace said as he headed for the door too.

"Dad don't worry Ro will be okay. I will talk to him about your lady situation and he will come around." Ray said giving me a hug and getting ready to head out behind Ace and Ro.

"Ray try and get your brother to let go of this Aja situation and let someone else handle it. I don't like how it can turn out." I said looking him in his eyes.

"I'll try Pops but he has it bad for that girl. I ain't never seen him like this."

He said shaking his head and heading out the door.

I picked up my phone and dialed April's number. After three rings she picked up.

"Hello?" she answered.

"April I need to talk to you about Aja and Ro. I will be there in fifteen minutes. Ace still got you at his safe house?" I said as I put the dishes in the dishwasher and straightened up to leave.

"Yes, but I'm on the way to the Starbucks on the corner meet me there." she said.

"Alright, I'll meet you."

I hung up and got my keys and my gun and put it in my side holster. I had a permit to carry so I wasn't worried about it being seen. All I know was that something had to be done because people in love do crazy things.

Chapter 8-Raymond

"Ray"

Man! That shit that just went down at Pops was crazy! I can't believe Pops is dating April of all people. I know he's been lonely these past few years so I figure their situation is temporary. That's why I didn't trip out once he told us. But

Ro on some other shit right now with the Pops situation and Aja. We definitely were going to talk when we got to his house.

I'm the family peace keeper so I always make sure things don't get out of hand between Pops and Ro. Those two are just alike crazy as hell and stubborn.

I've always been laid back like my moms. My mom's named me Raymond Lamont

Casey after Pops dad. She said he was her favorite out of Pops relatives.

Everybody says I look and act just like her. I am six feet two with a slim muscular build. I have hazel eyes, dark chocolate skin, and I kept my hair in a Caesar cut with my waves swimming. I can't wait to tell Kia what's going on between our parents. I hit her up on my phone and called my wifey. She answered immediately.

"Hey bae! How was breakfast with the crew?" Kia said.

"Man shit was crazy Ki Ki! Did you know Pops and April been dating? That's some fucked up shit Kia I could be fucking my sister if they get married! I said with a nasty look on my face.

"Boy you are crazy as hell we are not brother and sister. I knew about April seeing somebody but she didn't tell me it was your daddy. You know how April is.

She ain't serious about anybody. I give it a month and she will be on to the next victim." Akia said.

"I tried to tell Pops but you know how he is. Enough about them I need to see my baby so I will pick you up from the safe house after I leave from my brother's house." I said pulling into the driveway right behind Ace and Ro.

"That's fine bae I can't wait. Tell Ace to bring Aja over too I missed her so much while she was away." Akia said in an excited tone.

I could tell my babies deep as dimples were on full display through the phone.

"I'll try my best but my brother is holding her hostage right now. Let me go in here and see if I can stop world war four from happening between Ace and Ro."

I said taking off my seatbelt.

"What the hell is Ro doing with my sister? Baby, you need me to come over for backup?" She asked.

Kia was my ride or die. She always had my back no matter what. I have been in love with Kia ever since she smacked the shit out of me in the club when we first met. Yeah, I didn't know

109

at the time she was Ace's sister and all I saw was this fine ass slim thick hottie in a red bandage dress that had her ass sitting just right.

I saw her hanging out with her best friend Sabrina and everybody knows that Sabrina is down for any and everything. So, I assumed that hoes flocked together. Boy was I wrong! I came up behind her and put my hand on her ass. The next thing I know I had a hand print on my cheek. I apologized because I was wrong and man enough to admit it.

I didn't see her again until Ace invited me to a cookout and introduced me
to his sister. That night we hung out by the pool and just talked. After that we talked all the time on the phone and was constantly texting each other. We have been going strong ever since.

Ace would kill me if he knew that his sister had gone into my family business. She has been training with Ro to be on the hit squad. I tried to talk her ass out of doing it and going to college but she said school was never her thing.

Ace should have known that Akia was going to be part of the D-City Boyz. She hung out with us and Ace used her when he needed to get information out of women. She was his female enforcer. She begged Ro and me to teach her how to become a trained killer because she wanted to make her own money. Ace and I both gave her anything she wanted but she wasn't having it. She said she never wanted to be like April and depend on a man.

"Hello bae? You still there?" Akia yelled shaking me out of my thoughts.

"You know what, yeah slide through Kia because judging by the looks on Ace and Ro's face it's about to be some shit." I said shaking my head and looking at the standing there going back and forth yelling at each other.

"Ok bae I'm on my way, love you." Akia said.

"I love you to Ki be careful." I said hanging up and stepping out of my truck.

"Ro I told you I don't want you fucking with my sister! You used to them hoes like Tyesha and my sister not no hoe, so you need to back the fuck up!" Ace said getting in Ro's space which is something he usually didn't do.

But, when it came to his sisters that nigga was the terminator.

"Ace you my boy but no man can tell me what the fuck to do! Aja is my responsibility now and you can fall back and let me handle the situation!" Ro said through his teeth with a growl.

"Besides you can't tell me to stop fucking with her when I already have fucked her! That means she's mine now and she ain't leaving this house!" Ro yelled.

Oh shit! This wasn't good at all. Before I could get to them Ace had two pieced Ro and then the battle was on. They were trading shots back and forth. I could tell Ro was holding back because my brother is a black belt and trained in several forms of defense. As I was trying to break them apart Kia pulled up and

Aja and Kyra were coming out of the house.

"What the hell are they fighting for?" Kyra yelled.

I saw Aja running towards the scene to break it up.

"Aja stay back! I got it!" Kia yelled she pulled her gun and shot in the air.

Ace and Ro broke apart. I stood in the middle just in case they decided to go at it again. Ro and Ace were still standing staring each other down breathing heavy.

"What the hell are you two doing out here fighting like y'all aren't boys!" Kyra yelled.

"Aja why you going around sleeping with mutherfuckers you just met?! Is this what you been doing for the past four years? Fucking random mutherfuckers!!" Ace yelled.

Ro charged but before he could Aja walked over and smacked the shit out of Ace and Ro. They both looked at her. Ace looked shocked but Ro had that weird ass smirk on his face.

"Ace you have lost your damn mind talking to me like that! I am good and damn grown and can fuck who I want too! Now the next time you talk to me like that I'm going to shoot you in the ass for being an asshole!" She said and then turned to Ro.

"I don't know why you got that damn smirk on your face out here telling my damn business! I'm not Tyesha I will fuck you up, Ro!! Keep telling shit and you won't ever taste this again!! Kyra and Kia come in the house so we can get a drink before I really go off out here!" Aja said as she stomped in the house.

Kyra and Kia followed behind her shaking their heads.

"She told y'all asses!! That's my big sis right there!" Kia said laughing and closing the door.

Ro busted out laughing. Something that scared the shit out of me and I hadn't heard since before mama died.

"Ace I'm sorry for saying that shit man but you see that woman right there is going to be mine."

He walked towards the door smiling as he passed me and mumbled, "She got my shit hard as fuck bossing up on a nigga."

I'm glad Ace didn't hear what he said or they would be fighting again. Ace took a breath and calmed down after Ro went in.

"Why both of you mutherfuckers got to have my sisters! He asked.

"Man at least you know your sisters are with some real men and not these fuck boys out here.

You know Ro don't know how to express himself so it comes out fucked up. You know he's right about being able to protect her though. We still don't know who was shooting at us last night." I said starting to walk towards the house.

I needed a drink myself after dealing with these two hot-headed fools.

"I got some information on that situation before breakfast this morning.

We need to go down to Ro's man cave once we get a drink." He said walking beside me.

"Ace are you going to be cool with Ro dating your sister? I know how protective you are over her, especially after all the shit she's been through."

I had to ask because we needed to be on the same page with people coming at us.

"I know Ro and he's not a relationship type man. You and Kia are two of a kind so I don't worry as much. But Ro is hard and crazy as hell.

My sister might seem hard on the outside but she's fragile as hell. That sick as man has my sister shook. She has nightmares and shit behind him. I'm surprised she even let Ro near her let alone have sex." He said looking discouraged.

I put my hand on the doorknob and looked back at Ace.

"That should tell you something right there Ace. He must make her feel protected if she is letting her walls down. Now granted you are right and Ro don't usually do relationships but you also know that he doesn't lie. If he says he got her and she's his, then you know it's not a damn thing anybody can do to stop him. You trust Ro with your life everyday so you should trust him with your sister.

They might be good for each other. They both are fucked up in the head behind some shit and maybe they can be there for each other. Now put that shit out your mind and let's get up with Ro about rolling up on these mutherfuckers that are gunning for us."

I opened the door and the girls were in the kitchen drinking on some wine sitting around the island. I peeped Ro sitting at the table nursing a beer and taking peeks at Aja. I came up behind Kia and kissed her on her neck. She tilted her head so I could kiss those soft ass lips of hers.

"Damn sis please tell me this is not your man! Aja said putting her glass down.

"Yes, this is my bae right here. We are getting married in two months and I want you to be my maid of honor." Kia smiled showing off her five carat princess cut yellow diamond engagement ring.

"Of course I will baby sis!! I am so happy!! Aja said starting to cry.

They started hugging and talking about the wedding plans with Kyra. Ace looked at Ro and me and nodded for us to go downstairs. Ro sat his beer down and walked over to Aja. He stood in front of her and stared down at her. She was staring back.

"I'm sorry about saying something to your brother baby girl." He stared for a few more minutes and rubbed her cheek and walked down into the basement.

"Your damn brother is weird as hell!" Ace said shaking his head.

Come on let's go downstairs. Y'all stay up here and don't go anywhere." Ace said headed towards the stairs.

Kyra rolled her eyes and sucked her teeth. Ace stopped mid step and turned back around to her and got in her face.

"You got a problem Kyra? You sucking your teeth like you got something to say."

Kia, Aja, and I stared at them for a minute wondering what the hell was going on between these two.

"Get out of my face Ace; I can do whatever the hell I want. You not my damn daddy!" Kyra said rolling her neck.

"See what happens Ky if you take your ass out that damn door! Oh and by the way, I might not be your daddy but you used to call me daddy!" Ace said and turned around and went down the steps leaving Kyra standing there with her mouth wide open.

"Damn!" That's all I could say as I followed Ace downstairs to the man cave.

This day just keeps getting better and better.

Chapter 9-Akia

Aja and I just sat there and stared as Ace and Ray went downstairs.

"Kyra is there something you want to tell your best friend?" Aja said with a smile on her face.

"Aja I'm sorry we used to date back before you went through everything but we broke up. He was heavy in the streets and didn't want anyone to come after me since they were at war." She said.

"So you were the one that broke my brother's heart. His ass sulked around for months!" I said side eyeing Kyra.

I thought it was wrong as hell that she never told Aja about dating my brother and they were supposed to be best friends.

"I'm sorry he was hurt but it wouldn't have worked out." Kyra said as she opened the fridge and started looking through it.

There was something off about the way she said it like she was hiding some shit. Ever since I started training with Ro my senses had gotten better and I have picked up skills to tell when someone was lying. I am not sure what the hell is going on with Kyra and Ace but I damn sure going to find out. I turned to Aja who seemed to be in deep thought.

"Sis you okay? You look like you were in deep thought." I asked.

Aja sighed and ran her fingers through her hair. "I was just thinking about all the shit that has gone down in the past twenty four hours since I've been home. First, Tyesha acting crazy in the club, then the shooting, having sex with Ro, Ace and Ro fighting, and now finding out my best friend has been keeping secrets. My damn head is hurting now! "She said shaking her head.

"Aja I didn't mean to keep anything from you, it's just complicated. You know I love you and trust you with my life. I can't talk about it right now because it's too much for me to handle at the moment." Kyra said while fixing herself another drink.

"I need something to eat and Ro and got shit in here." she said looking disgusted.

"You know your man said we can't go anywhere Ky." I said being messy as hell.

Kyra rolled her eyes at me.

"Fuck Ace I want some Swett's. Some turnip greens, yams, and fried chicken." She said licking her lips.

"Oh girl yes I want those smothered pork chops. Fuck it grab Ace's keys so we can go!" Aja said grabbing her purse.

I was hungry as hell so I followed they asses right out the door too. I know the men will kick our ass once they figure out we're gone but I knew how to protect myself and my sister.

Protecting her was my job too because I didn't want her to leave again.

We all went through hell together growing up and had never been apart until Aja was kidnapped. When she went away to college I cried almost every night missing her but felt she would be safe but we were all wrong. She was raped and had to go into hiding. Ace watched me like a hawk once Aja went into hiding.

I felt like a prisoner going from school to home with one of his workers playing bodyguard. I didn't date until I started messing with Ray. Now don't get me wrong I messed around with a few of my bodyguards because I was curious about sex. I gave up my virginity to one of them and regretted every two minutes and five seconds it lasted.

He wanted to get serious and be my man but even with it being my first time I knew his shit was supposed to be bigger than that. My first time didn't hurt because his dick was literally the size of a Vienna sausage. The second guard I messed with broke my heart.

Ray was the third man to ever be inside my body. He was my bae and I loved every bit of his nine inches which is why I was pregnant now. I hadn't told anybody yet, I found out yesterday after a trip to the doctor. Ray and I said we wanted to wait a couple of years after we were married to have kids but my ass just had to get pregnant. I have no idea how he's going to act when he finds out.

Just as I had that thought about the baby we were pulling up to Swett's. We got out and got in line with our trays to get our food. This baby had me eating everything. I grabbed a slice of lemon pie, pot roast, turnip greens, macaroni and cheese, and hot water cornbread. I also got a large sweet tea. Once we paid we took our trays to a table and sat down.

"Kia I thought you hated green vegetables?" Aja asked.

I couldn't tell her that it wasn't me but her niece or nephew wanting these greens.

"I have grown to like a few green vegetables since you have been away. I am just glad to have you back." I said.

"Me too little sis I just hate that it had to be under the circumstances." Aja said cutting up her smothered pork chops.

I looked at her with a confused look on my face.

"What circumstances? "

"April called me and said that she was sick and needed me to come home right away. I can't believe all that drinking has finally caught up to her." Aja said shaking her head.

Kyra rubbed her back and I sat there in shock. There was nothing wrong with April's trifling ass! Why the hell would she tell Aja some shit like that! It then dawned on me that our own damn mama was setting my sister up.

I started looking around and checking my surroundings without being obvious. There were families, couples, and a few other people enjoying their meals but nothing out of the ordinary. Then my eyes fell on a table with two men that only had drinks on it. One of the men kept glancing at our table and the other one was looking out the window into the parking lot. My gut was telling me that they were after us. I got out my cell phone and texted Ray to call me while Kyra and Aja were eating. Not five seconds after I sent it he was calling me back.

"Ki Ki where you at? You know Ace and Ro over here going crazy as shit about y'all leaving the house!! You could…"

I interrupted him before he could continue going off.

127

"Hey Bae yes I know you miss me! I told you I was hungry and wanted some Swett's. I can order you a to-go plate. Maybe the fried shrimp that you love." I said in a cheerful voice so if anyone around was listening they wouldn't catch on.

See Ray was allergic to shellfish so he told me to use it if I was in a dangerous situation and needed help.

"Akia hold on Bae we are on our way! Hold up Ro wants you." Ray said handing the phone to Ro.

"How many Kia?" he asked in a calm even voice.

"I left two beers in the fridge but there could be some more in the garage outside." I said.

"Okay listen I need y'all to stay put inside until we get there. It shouldn't be but about twenty minutes. Are you strapped? How's Aja?" he asked.

"Of course baby I am always prepared. My sis and Kyra are tearing up this food." I said trying to laugh off the situation.

"Ok Kia if they make a move do what you have to do. I've trained you well.

Follow your instincts." he said.

Just then the door opened and Tyesha and her crew walked in. I knew all hell was about to break loose.

"Bae I have to go my friend Tyesha just walked in with her crew I'll talk to you later."

"Aw shit Ace step on it Tyesha is there too." Ro said hanging up the phone.

I placed my cell phone in my purse and took my two custom glocks and put them in reach under the table.

"Aja and Kyra some shit is about to go down and if anyone starts shooting I want you to head behind me to the back door through the kitchen." I said in a low voice that only they could hear.

They both looked around and spotted Tyesha and her band of thots.

"I see my sister wants her ass beat again!" Kyra said taking off her earrings.

About that time Tyesha spotted us and headed to our table. I was watching her but also watching the men at the table because they were the real threat. My sister was quiet but deadly with her hands so I knew she could handle Tyesha.

"You got some nerve leaving the club with my man last night hoe! She said yelling at my sister.

"Yes, I left with your man and took real good care of him last night! If you have a problem with that you need to address him! I will give you to the count of five to get the fuck out of my face before you swallow them fucked up ass yellow teeth in your mouth! "Aja stood up getting in Tyesha's face and started counting.

The men I had my eye on started easing something under the table. I knew what time it was and I knew the guys wouldn't make it here in time.

"Aja and Kyra I don't feel so good take me to the bathroom." I said holding my stomach.

Aja bumped past Tyesha and came to my side while Kyra wrapped her arm around my shoulders and helped me to the bathroom. I watched the men at the table motion for someone to come in. I also watched Tyesha spit in our food. I was going to get that bitch but first I had to figure out how the hell to get us out of here.

Once we got to the bathroom I locked the door.

"Kia what's going on?" Aja said.

"There are some men outside that I think are after us. I have never seen them before. I called the guys and they are on the way but I'm not sure they will get here in time." I said as I got out my glocks from my purse.

I looked over and watched both Kyra and Aja getting a gun out of each of their purses.

"Do you ladies know how to use them?" I asked.

"Yeah Ace makes us go to the range once a week for practice and once a week for self-defense." Aja said as she took the safety off her Bodyguard 380.

"Okay first let's see if we can find a way out of here."

We started looking around in the stalls.

"There's a door back here in the cleaning closet but I'm not sure where it leads." Kyra yelled.

She jiggled the knob but it was locked. I pulled out my lock kit from purse and picked the lock and slowly opened the door to peek around. I saw the door lead out to the alley.

"Ok we can get out this way but I'm not sure where it leads. If we can get to the car we can get the hell out of here." I said in a low voice.

Someone started knocking on the door.

"We'll be out in a minute!" Aja yelled.

"Okay I will go out first and y'all follow me out." I whispered.

I went out the door and eased down the alley. Once I got to the end I saw that we were on the side of the parking lot which was good because the car was only a few feet away. The bad part was we would have to pass the window where the men were sitting. I turned around and Aja and Kyra were behind my with their guns pointed towards the ground. My phone started vibrating and it was Ray. I answered the phone in a low voice but still watching my surroundings.

"Ray how close are you?" I asked.

"We should be pulling up in five minutes what's going on?" he asked in a concerned tone.

"We had to go out the back to the alley. They were about to make a move. We aren't far from the car. We might have to make a run for it."

Just as I said that a bullet went past my head into the brick wall.

Pow! Pow! Pow!

I ducked down and turned towards the door we just came out of and started shooting along with Kyra and Aja.

"Kyra run to the car and pull it over here. We'll cover you." Aja said.

My sister wasn't as shy as I thought she was. She sent a headshot to one of the men that was at the table. Kyra got to the car and gunned it to the entrance of the alley. About that time 4 more men came through the door firing.

"Aja get to the car I'm right behind you!" I yelled still firing.

"I'm not leaving you let's both go!" she said pulling me by the arm.

We were almost to the car when I felt a sting to my back and then it started burning. I knew I had gotten hit. I fell to the ground. Aja stopped and started back towards me and covered me with her body while still firing back shots.

"Aja go!! I'll be okay!" I said trying to reassure her and get her to safety but I knew she wouldn't go and I felt myself getting weak.

"I'm not going anywhere. Hand me your gun!" she said taking it and firing back. I heard tires screeching and more shots being fired. I heard my sister yell out Ace's name and I knew they had gotten there.

"Hang on sis help is coming." Aja said sounding pained. I looked at her and saw she had blood coming from her shoulder and a hole in her top.

"Aja you've been hit! I said trying to hang on.

I looked around and saw Kyra, Ace, and Ro shooting the rest of the men and Ray running towards Aja and I.

"Kia baby where are you hit at?" He said with tears in his eyes.

"My back and Aja is hit too." I said weakly the darkness was closing in on me.

The gunfire stopped and I heard footsteps. I looked at Aja and she smiled at me right before she passed out.

"Hell naw not both my sisters!! Ace screamed.

Ro was kneeling beside Aja checking out her body to see where she was hit.

Kyra was crying.

"Ace she's still breathing it looks like she got hit twice once in the shoulder and once in the side. We need to get them both out of here the cops are coming!

Ace call Doc Murphy and tell him to meet us at the Percy Priest safe house."

He gently lifted up Aja and carried her to Ray's truck.

"Baby I'm going to pick you up and it's going to hurt. I just need you to hang on for me alright Ki? He said softly.

I shook my head that I understood and braced myself for the pain as he lifted me in his arms. He placed me in the back beside Aja and Ro got in the driver's seat and took off while Kyra and Ace followed us in the car. I knew I was about to pass out but I needed to let Ray know what was going on. I prayed God would spare our baby.

"Ray I need to tell you something." I said holding his hand.

"Kia baby save your strength we gonna get you and your sister right as soon as we get to the house.

"Ray no listen to me, I'm pregnant." I said watching his face."

He looked shocked and put his head down.

"Damn sis! Congrats!" Ro said from the front seat.

Ray lifted his head and stared at me and a slow smile eased across his face.

He lowered his head and gave me the sweetest kiss on my lips.

"You got my future in you Ki so you know you need to make it. He or she is just like us, strong as hell." He said and held my hand. I could no longer hold on I fell into the darkness.

Chapter 10-Ro

We pulled up to the house and Doc Murphy and his team were standing by waiting on us. We had safe houses all over the city and each one had medical equipment for situations like this. I helped Doc Murphy with a problem three years ago and he became our on call doctor when any of the crew needed help. I ran to the back as they were lifting out Kia and then Aja and taking them into the house. I had the garage turned into an ER room and that's where they took Aja and Kia.

"Doc Kia is pregnant so be careful with what you give her." Ray said.

Doc shook his head and ran back into the garage along with three nurses that assisted him. Ray and I went to the den to get a drink and wait to hear what Doc had to say. Ace and Kyra came in the door not to long after I started pouring up glasses of Hennessy for everybody because it was going to be a long night and tensions were running high.

"Doc say anything yet about my sister?" Ace asked.

"He's working on them both now. We should know something shortly. Kyra tell me what the fuck happened at the restaurant?" I said sitting on the sectional after handing everyone a glass.

"I don't know a lot because Aja and I were arguing with Tyesha. Kia said she was feeling sick and asked us to take her to the bathroom. When we got there she locked us in and told us about some men at another table that she said were watching us. I found a door in one of the bathroom stalls and Kia picked the lock and we went out to try and sneak into the car. I don't know how they knew we were out in the alley but they followed us and started shooting. I ran to get the car and Aja and Kia stayed to cover me. I tried to get to them as soon as I could and saw them running to the car when Kia went down. Aja turned around and tried to help and that's when you all pulled up. This shit is fucked up! We have only been in town for two days and have been shot at twice!" Kyra said with tears coming down her face.

"Ky it will be okay. We gonna find out who these mutherfuckers are and make sure they don't fuck with y'all no more." Ace said rubbing Kyra's hand.

That made me remember that Ace was going to tell us what he found out this morning about the club shooting but we got a call about the girls and headed out.

"Ace man what did your source find out?" I asked.

"Man, it was Sabrina who I met up with. She texted me and said she had some info on the shooting. I get over there and this bitch comes to the door in her panties and nothing else. I told her thot ass to put on some clothes or she wasn't getting a dime. She had the whole apartment smelling like a three piece fish special at Captain D's." Ace said.

"So she didn't know shit?" Ray asked.

"She said there were four shooters and she heard one of them being called Talley. I got Tan checking to see what he can find out about anybody with that name." Ace said talking and turning up his glass.

"Good we need to know what the fuck is going on. Let me text Tan and have him pull the tapes from the restaurant to see if we recognize anybody." I said pulling out my phone.

After texting Tan we turned on the TV waiting to hear from Doc about our girls. All I kept seeing in my head was Aja in my arms bleeding. For that someone was going to pay severely and slowly. It was fucking with me heavy because I promised her I would keep her safe and she ended up with bullet holes. I heard footsteps in the hall and Doc came in with blood on his scrubs.

"They both will be fine. Akia was shot in the lower side of her back which went straight through. She lost a lot of blood but the bullet didn't hit anything major. The baby seems to be fine but I don't have the equipment here for an ultrasound. I suggest you take her to her OB-GYN tomorrow to check on the baby.

I gave her a transfusion and she should be fine. Aja was hit in the shoulder and her right side. The bullet went through her shoulder and out but the one in her side we had to get out. We stopped the bleeding and she should be fine. They both need to rest for the next two to three weeks if possible. Especially Akia with her pregnancy." Doc said.

"Man thank you Doc for taking care of my girl and her sister. We will have someone drop off that bag for you and your peeps." Ray said with a grin on his face.

After everyone thanked Doc I had one more question to ask, "Doc can we move them to another location?"

Doc thought about it for a minute and said, "Yeah, as long as you are careful with them. I will check on them later today and of course the nurses will watch over them until you move them." he said as he headed to the door.

"We need to move the girls away for a few weeks so we can let them recuperate. I say we order the jet up and take them somewhere. I have the house down in Punta Cana. We can head down there. Let me call Tyce and get things rolling. Y'all go see the girls and I'll be there in a minute." I said dialing Tyce's number.

"I'll have Tan cover things for us here while we're gone." Ace said as Kyra, Ray and he headed to the garage.

After calling Tyce and setting everything up I poured myself another drink before I went in to see Aja. I have never felt guilty about any shit that I've done but I felt like I failed her when she got shot. I finished my drink and headed to check on Aja.

Aja

Being shot hurt like hell! I never wanted to be in this position again but I would if it meant saving my sister. It had been two days since the shooting and we were on a private jet headed out of the country. Kia and I were in the bedroom of the jet on two beds. She was asleep and I was sitting up thinking about everything that was going on. No one would let us get up and do anything and I was bored as hell. Ro had been quiet and not really talking much to me and I wondered if he was mad at me for going out without telling them. Ace cussed Kia and I out for leaving the house. I just thank God that we were okay. Kia and the baby were both healthy and alive and so was I. My shoulder was stiff and my side hurt every time I moved but it could have been much worse. I was in deep thought when I heard a soft knock.

"Come in." I said softly so I didn't wake up Kia. Ro came in the door smelling good and looking fine with a white fitted T- Shirt and black joggers on.

"I just came to check on you and see how you are doing, baby girl." He said sitting on the foot of my bed.

"I'm doing okay just bored and tired of being in the bed." I said as he stared into space for a minute.

"Ro are you okay? I mean I know all of you are upset we didn't listen about going out but you have been giving me the silent treatment for the past few days." I said.

Ro rubbed his hand down his face and looked away again for a minute. He finally turned to me and grabbed my hand.

"Baby girl I'm not mad at you I'm mad at myself for not protecting you.

Seeing you covered in blood fucked with me. I'm not used to failing. I kill and protect people for a living. That's what I've always been good at. What I'm not good at is these damn feelings that you bringing on in me. I'm not right in the head baby girl and I'm not sure how to make this work. I ain't never had no relationship just fuck buddies." He said with a serious face.

I looked at him and knew he meant every word he said. I can't believe he is blaming himself.

"Ro listen, I don't fault you for what happened to me. People get hurt every day and you can't be with me every second of every day. I know what you all do for a living and there will always be enemies. Hell, look at me I'm not even doing anything illegal and I have some psycho after me. I trust you with my life, Ro please don't doubt that." I said leaning over and kissing him softly on the lips.

The kiss started off light but then he deepened it by invading my mouth with his tongue. He tasted like Hennessy and the Kush I know he had been smoking earlier. He gently laid me back and raised my dress. I wasn't wearing any panties so his fingers had easy access to my honeypot. When he slipped the first one in I moaned. The second finger went in and he started licking and sucking on my nipples.

"Shit Ro!" I called.

"I just know y'all nasty asses ain't trying to fuck while I am in this room!"

Akia said.

Ro and I jumped apart like we were on fire. Akia started laughing.

"Don't be ashamed now that y'all got caught. I'm getting up and going to sit in my man's lap and get felt up too!" Akia said throwing up deuces at us as she left out.

I was so embarrassed we got caught up and forgot that she was in the room.

"Well baby girl I guess we need to talk about what all this means. I would like to get to know you better since we will be staying in the Dominican Republic for a few weeks. Like I said before I come with a lot of shit I ain't gonna lie. I will do my best by you but know a nigga will fuck up until I learn." Ro said while rubbing the back of my hand.

"I can live with that Ro. I haven't been in a lot of relationships either with all that has been going on these past four years so we can learn together." I said.

Ro looked at me and his lips curved in a slight smile. We stared at each other and I leaned over to place a kiss on his mouth when the door banged open.

Ace stood in the doorway with a scowl on his face.

"I thought you said you was just coming in here to check on Aja not tongue her down! Look I know you all done did some shit but can you please not do that shit while I'm on this plane! Plus, she needs to be resting!" He stared us both down with a look of disgust.

"Baby girl I know you don't want to be cooped up in here come out to the front of the jet and we can sit and talk." Ro said still holding my hand.

I smiled because he hadn't let it go even though my brother was staring at us like he wanted to kill us both.

"Sure we can do that."

He helped me up and we walked past my brother. As we passed him he whispered in my ear. "Be careful sis there's more to Ro than you know."

I saw the worry on my brother's face as I followed Ro to the plush leather seats and sat down beside him. I looked over and saw that Ray and Kia were hugged up asleep with Kia in his lap and his hand on her still flat stomach. They made such a cute couple. I am so glad my sister has a man that clearly loves her to no end. I hoped Ro and I could get to that point. I looked over at Ace and Kyra and they sat across from each other stealing glances but not saying anything. I felt Ro place his hand on my thigh and I turned towards him.

We talked for the next two hours about our likes and dislikes. I noticed that no matter what, Ro had to touch me, and I loved every minute of it. He told me

about his mom and also about being an enforcer. I wasn't shocked by his profession since I knew he was a leader in the D-City Boyz. I told him about

Desmond and Tyler and about my years in hiding. We talked about everything in those two hours but I still felt like he was holding something back. I figured I would not pry too much since we were just getting to know each other but there was one thing I had to know.

"So what are you going to do about Tyesha? I know that we haven't put a title to what we are, but I refuse to be a part of a love triangle. I have been through too much for that. Plus the way her mouth is I will be up under the jail for killing her hoe ass!" I said to him.

I was not playing. That chick has always had something against me and I'm not sure what. What I do know is I was not the same quiet girl she knew back in school. Kyra's sister or not I would fuck her up if she messed with me.

"Aja I know how she is, believe me. Once we get back into town I will have a sit down with her and let her know what the situation is. I don't play games I'm a straight forward type of cat. I don't give a fuck what no one has to say about it.

So believe me when I tell you she will be dealt with and won't be a problem." Ro said sincerely.

I knew what he was saying but I also know Tyesha. I had a feeling that she was going to be a major problem in our relationship. The attendant came over the speaker and told us to buckle up since we were about to land. I looked out the window at the beautiful island that would be my home for the next few weeks and prayed that we all would find some peace for just a little while.

My mind and body were tired. I couldn't help but think about what was waiting for us when we came back. I couldn't help to wonder if he knew I was back in town. The thought instantly made me shiver and my heart race with anxiety. Ro must have sensed something was off because he got up and retrieved a blanket out of the storage compartment and covered me up. He then grabbed my hand and held it. I looked at him with a smile and instantly felt better. I'm not sure what we were starting, but I was loving everything about Mister Ro so far.

Unknown

I had been staking out Ro's house for a few days now and nothing. Dammit!

How the hell did they get away from me? Fucking around with that bitch Tyesha threw me off my game. Yeah, Tyesha knows exactly who I am and what I want.

She was supposed to help me get Aja from Swett's but the bitch fucked that up! I hated that I would have to wait to get my Angel but I will have her, no matter who is in the way. I pulled out my phone and dialed Tyesha's number.

"Hello?" she said.

"Bitch I gave you one damn job and you can't even do that shit right!

Where are they Tyesha?" I screamed in the phone.

"I don't know! It wasn't my fault I promise! I didn't know Derrick was having someone follow them!" Tyesha cried.

"Fuck your tears Tyesha! I want you to find out where they are. You fucking the nigga you should know where Ro is! You have one hour to find out and hit me back. If not you already know what the fuck I will do to you." I hung up on her ass before she could say another word.

Things were getting complicated with this damn war that Derrick wanted to start and finding out that my angel was under Ro's protection. I headed towards my house to smoke one and get a little Crown in my system. Once I got to the house and got my drink I went to the room I had for my queen. I left it just like before all white furniture with white silk sheets and fur carpet. It cost me a grip because everything was designer but she was worth it.

I walked into her closet that I had upgraded with new clothes since my baby had gotten a little thicker in all the right places. I even had her iced out with jewelry when she arrived. After sitting on the bed reminiscing about the first time I tasted her in this room, I got up and went next door to my seeds room that I had decorated in a circus theme since I didn't know if Aja gave birth to my son or daughter.

I went to my theatre room poured another glass of Crown and lit my blunt. I couldn't wait to get my angel home where she belonged.

Chapter 11-April

I was sitting in the bathtub with Luther playing in the background and candles lit all around. I had a big cup of my favorite Seagram's and was feeling real good. I was waiting on Rodney to get here with his dumb ass. The only reason I was messing with him was for his money. Plus we had plans for Rodney, his sons, and my kids. My kids gave up on me a long time ago so fuck them! I never wanted kids and here I go with three.

My family didn't believe in abortions because each birth meant more money. I heard footsteps coming down the hallway and I knew that meant Rodney was here.

"April where you at?" Rod called.

"Babe I'm in the bathroom." I said rolling my eyes getting ready to play my part.

Rodney walked in and sat on the toilet lid.

"We need to talk about this Ro and Aja thing. You know how complicated them being together will be. Ace is my son and I think it's time to let them know before things go too far between Ro and Aja." Rodney said looking at me daring me to say anything but yes.

I smiled on the inside because this was going better than I anticipated. I looked at him and rolled my eyes like I didn't want him to spill the secret and even started tearing up. I was about to win an award for this performance.

"No, Rodney you promised me that you wouldn't tell Ace about you being his father! This will kill my kids! Kia is engaged to Raymond and you didn't seem to have a problem with that!" I screamed.

Rodney rubbed his hand down his face in frustration.

"Look April I love you so I'm only telling you this because I trust you. Raymond is not my biological son. Evette had an affair and the result was Raymond. I forgave her and claimed Raymond as my own." He said looking down.

Now that was a shock to me! Rodney was messing around with Evette and me for years at the same time but it was never serious between us at least on his part. When I needed money he would hit me off and when he needed this good shit he came and got it.

"So since you found out that Aja is messing with your biological son Ro you want to tell Ace he's your son." I asked getting out of the tub and wiping my body down with a towel.

Rodney's eyes were all over my body which looked damn good at my age. I was light skin with black eyes that my son inherited from me. I stood at five feet six and weighed a curvy one hundred and fifty pounds. I started oiling my body with baby oil slowly. I watched him through the mirror licking his lips and I knew I had him right where I wanted him.

"Babe the kids went away and didn't tell me where they were going. If you want to stop Aja and Ro then we need to go and tell them in person." I said wrapping my arms around his neck and placing my naked body against his.

"You right baby, we need to stop them before it goes any further. Ro is already going crazy over your daughter and you know how unstable he can get. I don't want my son ending back up there seeing those head doctors." He said pulling me close.

"I agree. You find out where the kids went and I will pack us a bag so we can go tell them the truth." I said kissing him gently on the lips and walking into my closet.

Rodney walked off and started dialing numbers on his cell phone. I smiled and got out my cell phone and text my niece Tyesha telling her I would have the information for her in a few minutes. That's right Tyesha is my niece and she always treated me better than my own kids. My kids never met my family because I told them that they were dead. So they had no clue what I was really into. My brothers Doug and Damon needed me to help them pull off this plan and like the good little sister I was down to help. As long as they paid me my money we wouldn't have any problems.

"April the kids are down at Ro's beach house in Punta Cana. I called up the jet and we can leave in the morning. I just hope the boys understand why I have been keeping these secrets." He said shaking his head.

I needed to relax him so I dropped my towel and strutted over to him.

"Rodney they love you. No matter what you are their father and they will just have to accept it. Come on over here and let me take your mind off of everything Daddy." I said pulling him down on top of me.

As he nibbled on my neck I was thinking about my real man and pretending that Rodney was him so I would get wet. I also couldn't help but think about how proud my brothers and he would be of me. The plan was going well; the boys would be devastated and mad at Rodney causing a rift in the D-City Boyz. They would be so broken that no one would see their destruction coming. The thing is, Ace is not Rodney's son. It was all a part of the plan. Stupid ass nigga was so cocky he didn't even ask for a blood test.

My brothers and nephew would take over the city and Rodney, Ro, Ray, and Ace would be dead. Our family would be on top and I would be living the good life rich and doing what the fuck I wanted to do. I would deal with Akia myself with her bourgeois ass! I could be with my man out in the open and my man would get the one thing that he has always wanted, Aja.

Tyesha

"Uncle Damon Tee Tee April just text and said that they are in Punta Cana. I already texted my daddy and told him to meet us here to go over the plan." I said.

"Good job baby girl. Son, what the hell were you thinking shooting up the club and the restaurant! That's reckless as hell and will get your black ass thrown back in prison! We almost have everything we want just be patient and you can kill Ace once we have control." Damon said.

I kept trying to tell Derrick but his ass was hard-headed! I had just finished combing the girl's hair and braiding it and putting beads at the ends.

"Girl's go to your room and turn on Doc Mc Stuffins." I told them.

They immediately ran to their rooms. I didn't like talking business in front of them. I might be a fucked up person but I loved my girls and didn't want them to grow up fast like I did.

"Derrick you need to listen to your dad. It won't be long and you can get your revenge for Desmond." I said rubbing his back.

"Alright, Dad I got you. But, I want Ace and Aja to die." Derrick said with a determined look on his face.

"You can't have Aja son. She's already promised to the main man." Uncle Damon said. I could tell by the look on Derrick's face that he was not happy.

"Fuck him! He was the one that killed Desmond all because of that bitch! Why are you even working with someone that killed your own son?" Derrick screamed.

Damon got up and punched Derrick hard in his throat. Derrick instantly fell to the ground.

"Watch who the fuck you are talking to nigga! I'm your father and you should know I don't tolerate any disrespect! The reason I still deal with him is because that's where we get our money from! Your brother was told to get close but not too damn close but he had to start thinking with his dick! Now, I advise you to tighten up before you next on the list!"

Damon kicked Derrick in the side and started to walk off.

"Niece call main man and let him know where they at. Then pick your stupid ass husband off the floor and talk some sense into him."

He walked out of the door slamming it. I walked over to Derrick and tried to help him up but he pushed me away. I shook my head and went into the kitchen to text *Main* as we call him. He was rude as hell earlier on the phone and I was not about to call him and hear him threaten me about the shit that went down earlier. As soon as I sent the text he was responding back saying okay.

I got out some hamburger meat to make some hamburger helper because I didn't feel like cooking. I am glad Uncle Damon finally told him about Main killing Desmond but it just seemed to make Derrick angrier.

He had been taking out his anger on me and I was getting sick of the shit! I loved him but a bitch could only take so much! I will be glad when he got his revenge so he could get back to the man that I love. Speaking of which, I tried to call Ro again but his ass still had me on the blocked list. I was heated because I know he had that bitch in his bed! I can admit I was jealous as hell! I had been with him for two years and he never took me on a vacation!

Just then my aunt texted me and said to get packed and head to Punta Cana so I could help her with her plan. Yes!! This is just what I needed! A trip away from my husband and to fuck up the happy little trip Ro and Aja had planned. I knew just what I needed to do to help the situation along.

I finished cooking and texted Uncle Damon so he could come and get the girls after seeing Derrick turning up the whole bottle of Ciroc on the table. Shaking my head I went in the bedroom and started packing. Derrick followed me in and sat on the bed.

"Ty baby why are you packing?" he asked.

"I am going down to the DR to help TeeTee with her part of the plan. I should be back at the end of the week. Your daddy is on the way to get the girls." I said zipping up my suitcase. When I turned around Derrick grabbed me by the throat and slammed me into the wall.

"You bet not fuck that mutherfucker when you down there, Tyesha! I'm sick of having to share my wife!! He said through clenched teeth.

I tried to say yes but his grip was too strong around my neck. I shook my head to let him know I understood and he immediately dropped me to the floor and went out of the house slamming the door. I wiped the tears from my eyes and got up. I checked on the girls who had fallen asleep on their twin beds. I heard the key turn and Uncle Damon walked in.

"You ready to go?" he said I shook my head yes and let him help me place the suitcase in my car. I gave him a few last minute instructions on the girls and I was headed to the airport. I prayed this whole scheme would end soon.

Chapter 12-Ro

We had been in the DR for four days now and I had spent almost every moment getting to know Aja. We had been chilling by the pool of my 5 bedroom beach house that has a guest house in the back. It was one of four houses I had around the world. Being a hit-man meant I needed to have my bases covered in case shit went left on one of my missions.

Right now, I was waiting on one of my computer connects to get me some information on April. Kia came to me after we arrived and told me she thought April had something to do with what went down at the restaurant. I can't say it would surprise me if she did. We agreed that we would keep it from everyone especially Aja until we had more information. I was also looking into who her stalker was. I was going back gathering information from when he first surfaced.

I kept checking my email and phone to see if they had found out anything. Since I didn't see anything; I decided to call Pops and check on him and to let him know I was putting a hold on my missions until after this mess was over.

"Well if it isn't my runaway son." He said in his deep voice.

"What's up Pops I was just calling to check in and see how you are doing?" I said.

It's all good here son on my end just preparing to send some employees to clean up a spill." he said.

I knew that was code for sending out hitters on missions. My Pops had ten elite hitters on his team and we were sent all over the globe to handle situations. None of the jobs we did were less than five hundred thousand dollars each. The harder ones would cost you five million.

"Pops I need more time off to handle some business. Maybe two months tops." I said.

I decided to pull up Google and see what I could do special for Aja tonight. Yeah, a mutherfucker needed Google because I was not a relationship cat. I ordered her some calla lilies because she said that was her favorite flower. She hated roses all because her stalker always sent them.

"Ro did you hear what I said?" Pops asked.

"Sorry Pops I didn't, what you say? I said knowing he was going to light into my ass.

"You need to stop thinking with your little head and get your head back in the game. You over there messing around with Aja when you need to be figuring who is shooting at y'all. April and I need to talk to you all so we should be there tomorrow." Pops said.

I hoped like hell he wasn't coming to tell us that April and him were getting married or some shit. Because I was still wrapping my mind around them being together.

"Pops don't start with that Aja and I shit! No disrespect but I'm grown as hell and at least Aja ain't like April so you can kill that shit!" I screamed in the phone.

I felt myself getting to that point of upset where I black out and I didn't need that shit with Aja in the house. I tried to control my breathing and get it under control but it was hard as hell when I get to that point of darkness. Aja has so much shit going on in her life that I didn't want to bring her into my fucked up problems. My Pops must have sensed something wrong.

"Ro are you still with me?" he asked in a worried tone.

"I'm good Pops just hurry up and get her and say what you have to say. But I'm warning you; don't say shit about Aja and me." I said hanging up.

I was in the middle of counting and breathing when Aja walked in looking fine as hell in a green bikini and matching green wrap around her waist. She had bandages on from the shooting but it didn't matter. Her body was glowing all over and her hair was down and wavy. I knew she had just finished laying by the pool. Looking at her curvy body had my third leg leaking but I wasn't trying to take it there with me being so close to my darkness.

"I thought you were coming out to join me by the pool?" She said with her hands on her hips.

"I am baby girl I just had to take care of some business but I will be out in a few minutes. You want me to cook you something for lunch?" I said.

Cooking always relaxed me and helped calm my nerves.

"Baby you cook?" she asked with a smirk on her face.

"Hell yeah! I can throw down in the kitchen, baby girl. My mama taught me well." I said walking up on her and putting my hands on her waist.

"So what you want? I can make just about anything." I said smiling down at the beauty before me.

I then realized that my nerves had instantly calmed as soon as I touched her.

"Let's throw some steak and hot dogs on the grill. I can make the sides if you grill the meat." Aja said with a smile on her face.

One of the things that I have learned in the past few days is that Aja was laid back and sweet as hell. She was definitely wifey material and I was going to try my best to keep her as close to me as possible. She provided a much needed peace to my fucked up life. I could feel myself getting more and more attached and that was dangerous for both her and me. I wanted to tell her all my dark secrets but I didn't want to scare her away either.

"That sounds good. You go in the kitchen and get started and I will go and prep the grill." I said placing a soft kiss on her lips.

"Ummm you keep kissing me like that and we won't make it to the kitchen." She moaned against my lips.

I regretfully pulled away.

"You right about that baby girl. Take your fine ass in the kitchen and I'll wrap up stuff here and head out and start up the grill." I said.

She smiled and turned around and headed for the kitchen. I watched her walk away with that round ass booty that you couldn't help but look at. I went over and switched off my computer when my business phone rang. I looked down and saw it was Gunner. He was Tan's brother and our tech man. If you wanted some shit dug up he could hack anything and find out.

"Speak." I answered.

"Ro man I found out some shit but it can't be discussed over the phone. We need to meet up." Gunner said.

I ran my hand down my face because I knew it had to be some serious shit if we needed to talk in person. Gunner never wanted to leave his house. He was a recluse and we usually only got him out by going on missions and paying him a lot for tech support.

"Gunner, I'm out of the country but I will send Pops jet to pick you up at the airport and bring you here to me. I'll double your fee for the hassle man.

"Ro, no need with the information I have I would do this shit for free. I'm packing now." Gunner said in a tone that had me wondering what the fuck was going on.

"Say less." I hung up and texted the pilot and Gunner to let him know the pickup time.

I sat down at my desk because I was getting that uneasy feeling that something bad was coming. I was in deep thought when Ray and Ace walked in.

"What's good bro? The girls are in the kitchen looking like they are about to throw down! Aja said you about to throw some meat on the grill." Ray said and was about to say more when he saw the look on my face.

"What the hell is going on now? I know that look on your face Ro." Ace said.

They both sat down and waited for me to tell them what was going on. I ran down my conversation with Pops and Gunner.

"So, we have Pops and Gunner coming down to tell us more fucked up news! On one hand I'm curious to see what they have to say but I have a bad feeling we ain't gonna like what they have to say." Ray said.

I shook my head agreeing because I had the same feeling.

"I still have a few soldiers looking into some shit about the shooting at the club and restaurant. I also told Tan to keep an eye on April's crib and mine in case Aja's stalker sends some shit in case he has figured out she's back in town. I am glad she's here and not there right now because you were right, we got too much heat on us right now. The only problem I have with you and Aja being together is your temper. That blackout shit scares the fuck out of me when it comes to my sister being around you." Ace said with a serious look on his face.

"Have you told her about your problem Bro?" Ray asked.

I shifted uncomfortably in my seat because I knew my answer wasn't going to be what he wanted to hear. I just didn't want her to hear about my problem from her brother either so my answer had to be good.

"I haven't told her yet Ace. I want us to get to know each other better before I start laying out my dirty laundry. This isn't the kind of thing I can just spring on somebody. I have something special planned for her tonight so I will try and tell her then." I said to Ace but I still wasn't sure I was going to tell her.

"Just make sure you do, Ro. That's my heart and brother or not I will go to war over her." Ace said staring me down with a look of warning on his face.

All I could do was nod my head in understanding because I would do the same for my brother.

"So what your lunatic ass got planned, bro?" Ray asked.

I thought about some ideas I read about, "You know I'm not the romantic type but I figured I would take her for a late night picnic down by the ocean on the beach. You know candles and shit with some 90's joints playing from my phone. What y'all think?" I said uncertainly.

I hoped they wasn't about to clown me for this shit.

"Naw bro that's some panty dropping shit right there!" Ray said.

Ace looked at both of us with a scowl on his face.

"I'm about to bounce man! I don't want to hear shit about either of my sisters' panties!" He said getting up and walking out the door.

Ray laughed and I shook my head as he left.

"Bro for real though, Aja needs to know what's going on before y'all get too deep. Hell, you need to let Ace know about your condition. Have you been taken your meds?" he asked with a serious look on his face.

I started taking meds about five months ago. Ray was the only one that knew about it. My Pops wasn't a big believer in doctors and pills so he would go the fuck off if he knew.

"I haven't taken them in about a week. With all the shit that keeps popping up I forgot to get them." I said.

Ray stared at me for a moment and then leaned in closer.

"Ro, I love you man but you fucking up. You need to get them pills and start taking them ASAP. You got a niece or nephew on the way and I want you to be in his or her life. But, if you don't take your pills I can't have you flipping out around Kia. I know you definitely don't want to have an episode with Aja so please get Gunner to bring your meds with him down here. You know what you have to do so do that shit Ro. Now come on so we can fire up the grill." Ray said standing up.

I stood up to and grabbed my phone.

"I got you Ray I'll tell Gunner to get some from his sister Simone she's a nurse over at Meharry. She always leaves the labels off for me. Let's get out of here before the girls come looking for us." I said and we headed out to the patio overlooking the private beach area to join Ace who already had the charcoal lit and three beers waiting on us.

We sat around and chit chatted for a while after we had the meat on the grill. I had text Gunner about my meds and also setup my surprise for Aja tonight. I've never been one to get nervous but talking about my condition always had me shook.

The doctor finally put a name to it five months ago and I was still coming to terms with it. How am I going to tell Pops, Ace, and Aja this shit without them looking at me with fear in their eyes? My whole life changed with those few sentences the doctor spoke.

Mr. Casey your blackouts, explosive anger, and severe mood swings are all symptoms of Bipolar Disorder. We can help you control them with the right combination of medicine and therapy. I tuned everything out once she said those few sentences.

I always knew I was different but I didn't think I was that fucked up. She also told me that I had borderline psychopathic tendencies and a possible split personality. I laughed on the inside at that one because she had no clue what I did for a living and how much I enjoyed it. It explained a lot and the pills after helped keep the darkness at bay but it never truly got rid of my urges to kill. I used my job to help me with those. My problem now is telling Aja she was messing with a true monster. Who the fuck wants to be with a real psychopath? She would always fear me and I didn't want that. I wanted her to continue to look at me like her hero. I know I should let her go be with somebody normal but I couldn't let her go.

I craved her like no other. I prayed that I could keep the other side of me at bay until I got my meds. My brother is the only one that has met my other side. My father and other people have seen me during those times but they just chalk it up to it being my temper. I was brought out of my thoughts by the girls bringing out bowls of potato salad, baked beans, rolls, and fruit platters. I noticed Ray was taking the steaks and chicken off of the grill. Aja came and sat down on my lap with a smile.

"Ro, what you want to drink, another beer?" She said with a smile.

I shook my head yes and she got up to get it. I watched her through the glass laughing with Kia and Kyra about something. She was glowing and happy and I wanted to keep her that way. I just hoped my beast didn't scare my beauty away.

Unknown/Main

I watched from a distance with my binoculars as my angel came out putting food on the table and sitting on Ro's lap. It was supposed to be my lap she was sitting on not his. I have been watching the house from my boat since Tyesha told me where they went to. My angel was looking so good in her bikini and wrap that my shit bricked up immediately from the sight. I needed to do some digging because I never see Aja with our child. She bet not have gotten an abortion or I was going to kill Kia! I warned her so it would be her fault if she made me do it. Then I would drop my seeds in Aja again until she had my baby. Just thinking about it made my shit get harder.

"Tyesha!!! Bring your ass out here and suck this dick!!!" I yelled.

I really couldn't stand her ass or April's. They were a means to an end and that end was Aja. I was getting real tired of April's ass being clingy and shit. She had to be delusional if she thought I was going to keep her around after I had Aja. The day I saw them walking I didn't realize that it was April because I hadn't seen her in years. She had changed her hair color and gained some weight.

See years ago my Pops put me on to his secret business he had. Him and his partner Doug Sr. and his kids Damon and Doug Jr. kidnapped babies and young kids and sold them. They would sell them to anybody. Damon, Doug, and I took over the business after I killed my Pops. He was making millions but wanted to stop when he found out that Damon and Doug was keeping some of the kids for their sex ring. We couldn't allow that to happen so he had to die. Tyesha and April didn't know they had been kidnapped and were not family members. Doug Sr. kidnapped April from a store in Louisiana and brought her to Nashville because his wife wanted a little girl. He raised her like he did Damon and Doug Jr. to work in the family business. She helped us buy Tyesha from her crack head mama. April and I started messing around and she ended up pregnant with Ace. She says he's mine but I doubt she knows who her seed is by. Her brothers used to use her to set-up and rob dealers so she was sleeping with a lot of people back then.

After killing my Pops I had to lay low for a few years so when I came back April's appearance had changed. I got up with Damon and Doug Jr. and they told me about the plan to take over and I knew I wanted in on it. I had them set-up a meeting with April and started seducing her until I got what I wanted. She agreed and installed the cameras so that I could see my angel whenever I wanted. April's dumb ass thought the cameras were for her security.

I felt my zipper being pulled down and saw Tyesha on her knees pulling my third leg out and placing it in her mouth. Damn! Damon and Doug had trained her ass well on giving head! It's a good thing to because she was loose as hell. There was literally no bottom to her shit. After she finished me off I sent her ass back down to the bottom and focused on the task at hand. Getting my angel away from Ro. I wasn't scared of him but I knew his reputation. He would make it very difficult to get her while she was with him. I would have to watch and wait to see when I could get her alone. I brought Tyesha down to help me distract Ro so I could snatch Aja and take her home where she belonged. As soon as I had her I was killing April. She knew too much and I knew she would be salty when I married Aja.

April and Tyesha both know my true identity but I knew Tyesha wouldn't say shit because she had been trained not to. Plus Tyesha knew her place and wasn't emotional over me. I looked over again and watched everyone at the table eating and laughing not realizing that they were being watched. I needed to come up with a plan on how to get her without killing Ro. I had other plans for him.

Chapter 13-Ace

I was headed back to my room to change and go pickup Gunner from the airport when I bumped into Kyra. She lost her balance so I held her close so she wouldn't fall. Big mistake because her body was pressed into mine closely.

"Sorry I didn't see you." She said in her soft voice.

I looked into her gray eyes and got lost in them.

"It's alright Ky."

I looked down and noticed she was dressed like she was going out.

"Where you headed to?" I asked.

"I was going to the mall to pick-up a few souvenirs for my mom and AJ. She said while looking in her purse.

"Who the fuck is AJ?" I said walking up on her.

Even though she wasn't mine, my heart couldn't take it if she was in love with someone else.

"That's my mom's boyfriend which shouldn't matter to you Ace. Now back up off of me!" She said trying to push me and move me away.

I grabbed her ass and pushed her into my room. When she tried to get back out I grabbed her and dropped her on my bed. I immediately laid on top of her and held her arms over her head.

"Girl calm your ass down talking to me like you crazy!" I said in a low growl.

"Fuck you Ace you ain't my damn daddy! She said wiggling her body trying to get away from me.

"Oh I ain't daddy now huh! Let's see about that!

I started grinding into her and could feel her getting wet through her thin sundress she had on.

I could tell she didn't have on any underwear and I knew I had her. She struggled for a minute and that just made me grind harder. I started sucking on her neck and moved down to her breast slipping it out of her dress and bra. I licked around her nipple and started sucking on it like I was a newborn baby. I heard her moan and felt her legs spread wider.

I still had on my swim trunks so it was easy for me to take my mans out and push all nine inches into her tight treasure. I almost moaned myself when I felt how tight she was. I could tell she hadn't given my shit away. I started giving her long deep strokes once she got adjusted to me again. She started moaning and digging her nails into my back which she knew drove me crazy.

I felt myself about to blow so I flipped her over and she knew to get in the perfect arch position so I could watch her from behind. I started moving slowly just watching my mans disappear and come out covered in her cream. I noticed that ass had gotten fatter and she had a few stretch marks here and there. That shit turned me on even more because I knew she was all natural. Camille had ass implants and her ass was not soft at all.

I squeezed Ky's cheeks and pulled her towards me. She started throwing it back on me so tough I had to grab her around the waist to slow her down. I wrapped my arm around her stomach and felt a scar on it. I was going to ask her how it got there but she started going faster and I felt myself about to explode. I picked up my pace and she started getting wet as a waterfall. Next thing I know she was calling my name.

"Ace shit right there I am cumming! " She moaned.

I smacked her on her ass and said, "That's not my name when I'm in my pussy!"

I stopped and she groaned and screamed out, "Yes, Daddy that's my spot!"

I smiled and went in hard and fast hitting that spot just right until I felt her squirting all over my legs and sheets. I felt that rush that I only got from being in her and exploded all in her. My nut kept coming like a geyser until I was weak. We both collapsed afterwards and I pulled out and lay beside her. We were both sweaty and huffing. Her curly hair was all over her head and wet. I stared into her eyes and even though she hurt me I knew she would always have my heart.

"Ky I still love you. Why can't we be together?" I asked.

She looked at me with tears in her eyes. She huffed and got up and started putting her clothes back on.

"Ace I will always love you but we can never be together." She said looking at me one more time before she headed out the door taking another piece of my heart.

I laid back thinking about all the time that we spent together trying to piece together what I did wrong. I wasn't perfect, I did my dirt because I was young and dumb at the time and had the world at my feet. Something didn't seem right to me about the whole situation. Ky and I were supposed to be forever. I had her name tattooed over my heart.

My phone alarm went off letting me know it was almost time to pick-up Gunner from the airport. I needed to get my mind right and find out what the hell is going on in D-City. Big C passed the crown down to me but he still got a percentage and had say so if I continued to keep it. My phone beeped again and this time it was Camille calling.

"What up." I answered.

"Baby, when are you coming home? I miss you. Daddy said you had to go out of town." Camille said in her squeaky voice.

"Why you asking your pops about me? We don't know how he's going to react to that shit! You always being messy, Camille! Don't think I'm still not pissed about that scene you and your girl made in my club either." I said getting pissed all over again.

"Baby, it wasn't me it was Tyesha's ass doing all that! I didn't know that girl was your sister! Come on baby don't be mad at me. Daddy doesn't know anything about us. I really miss you." She cried.

I didn't love Camille like I did Ky. I kept her around because she was a good distraction from missing my other half. Don't get me wrong I cared about her but it wasn't love.

"Camille we can talk when I get back in town okay?" I said hoping it would get her off the phone.

"Okay baby that's all I ask. Love you!" Camille said sounding all excited.

"Yeah, alright." I said hanging up.

My love life was starting to be complicated. I needed to figure out how to get rid of Camille without getting killed for breaking her heart because Big C didn't play about his daughter. I also had to find a way to figure out what was going on with Kyra because I wasn't giving up on her being mine.

Kyra

I am so stupid for letting him touch me again! Here I was standing under the spray of the shower letting it wash away the evidence of my moment of weakness. There was still that delicious soreness and tingling between my thighs as I thought back to his touch. Even now I wanted to run to him and tell him everything if he would just hold me in his arms again. But, too much had happened for it to ever be the same. Once he found out the real reason I left, I knew he would hate me forever. If there was one thing Ace couldn't stand was betrayal and I was the queen of it.

I got out of the shower and dried myself off and started oiling my body. I wrapped a towel around my hair and my body and sat down on the bed to call my mom. She picked up after the first ring.

"What's wrong baby?" she asked.

She always knew when I was in trouble. I immediately broke down and started crying.

"Mom I fucked up! I tried to stay away from him but it's hard! I still love him so much!" I said in between sobs.

She sighed.

"Baby, I know it's hard but you have to stay strong. You have to keep your secret at all costs. You of all people know what will happen if the wrong people find out." She said.

I took a breath and told her to repeat the words I asked her to say when carrying this secret got to heavy. She went over the words I spoke to her the night that changed my life.

"We take this secret to the grave. I can't be selfish because it's not about me." I mouthed the words along with her.

I still felt horrible but at least talking to her reminded me of the bigger picture.

"Thanks mom, I really needed that. How's AJ?" I asked.

"Girl asleep!" She said laughing. "I'm about to get some work done while I can." My mom worked from home, processing insurance claims.

Aja and I also worked for the same company while we were in hiding using the fake ID's that Ace got us. We were saving so we could open up a fitness center or spa together.

"Okay mom I'll let you go. Please kiss AJ for me and I will call y'all tomorrow. Love you much!" I said.

"Love you much better!" she said before hanging up the phone.

It was a burden carrying secrets from those you love but I just couldn't take the chance of it all blowing up in my face. Aja and Ace would never forgive me and I couldn't deal with losing my best friend since I already lost the love of my life. I got dressed in a pair of PINK sweat pants and a matching sports bra. I sat out on the balcony and smoked some good Kush that I got from Ray earlier. I sipped on a glass of white wine and just watched the wave's crash on the beach. It was relaxing and was helping me to calm my nerves from the issues that were going on. I heard a knock on the door and got up to go unlock it praying it wasn't Ace.

"Who is it?" I called out.

"It's me, Aja." She said.

I opened the door and let my girl in. She had on a robe and it looked like she had just got out of the shower because her hair was wet and wavy.

"Ky I need some advice."

She said following me out to the balcony. I grabbed another wine glass on the way and poured her a glass as she sat down. I also lit another blunt and passed it to her.

"So, what's up Chica?" I asked.

She took a puff and slowly let the smoke out.

"You know I have only had two boyfriends Desmond and Ty. With both of them it took me a long time to trust and warm-up to them. With Ro, I feel so safe and secure and we have known each other less than a week. I don't know how to feel about it. I really like him a lot. I can feel myself falling for him fast and hard and it's literally scaring the hell out of me. I don't want to fall in love with him and have him taken away from me just like Tyler." Aja said with tears in her eyes.

I pulled my chair closer and grabbed her hand.

"Don't let your stalker stop you from living, Aja. He has already taken so much from you and it's time you take your life back. Don't lose out on a good man that cares about you because of fear. I see the way that man looks at you and caters to you. He is falling deep in love with you. Now wipe them damn tears before your man sees that shit and kills us all thinking we done something to his queen." I said laughing causing her to laugh too.

"He is a little extra." she said.

I had to look at her to see if she was serious because Ro was a whole lot more than extra. We laughed and talked until Ro texted her and said he had plans for them in a couple of hours. We said our goodnights and I was again alone to deal with the problems that seem to be ever present these days.

I wanted Ace and I to be making plans like Ro and Aja. Or sneaking off to get a quickie like Akia and Raymond but that wasn't in the cards for us. I finished off the bottle and climbed into bed to watch some good ol' ratchet TV to get my mind off of what I couldn't have and that was Ace. They say karma is a bitch and right now she was beating my ass. I prayed that my deeds would never come to the light and that my heart would heal eventually. As I was dozing off one famous quote kept running through my mind. "What's done in the dark always comes to the light."

Chapter 14-Ro

I was sitting in my man cave in the basement with Ray waiting on Ace and Gunner to come. My Pops had text me earlier and said something came up and he wouldn't be able to come until the end of the week. I thought that was odd because he was foaming at the mouth to come out and talk to us just this morning.

"Ray, you think something is up with Pops wanting to cancel on us like that?" I asked.

Ray rubbed his hand down his face and said, "Yeah, shit is a little suspect but maybe something came up with one of the missions or a shipment. You know Pops is covering for you and Kia and also handling getting in that big ass load of Kush coming in from the islands."

I shook my head agreeing but something seemed off to me. Before I could think on it more Ace and Gunner walked in and we all dapped each other up in greeting. Gunner pulled out his laptop and powered it up.

"Alright Gunner, what was so important that you had to see us in person to tell us?" Ace asked.

"Ro asked me to look into April and I found out some shit that goes deeper than I've ever seen before. I looked for a birth certificate for your mama and I can't find one. It looks like she just popped up on the radar when she gave birth to you. That's when her social security number started showing up in any systems and it belongs to a baby that died. I'm not sure who April is and if that's even her real name." Gunner said with a frown on his face.

We all had a shocked look on our face.

"April always has been shady but I didn't think she was shady enough to have a fake identity. But, here lately she has been real extra. She called Aja and told her she was sick and needed her to come home. The only kind of sick she has been is when she hasn't had a drink in a few hours. Then Kia said that she told April that they were going to the restaurant and then the girls get shot at. Something is going on with her." Ace said with a worried look on his face.

We all shook our head in agreement.

"That's not all either." Gunner said with an uneasy look on his face.

"What man just spit it out?" Ray said impatiently.

"I pulled every paper on her I could find but there was one important thing missing and one piece of paper that has me shook. I found birth certificates and Ace and Akia but there is no record anywhere of Aja being born. The records that are in the system are fake. Her social and birth certificate are very good fakes at that. Someone with some money had to get them. Now I had Tan go to April's house and lift some prints so we can run them and see who she really is. We should have the results tomorrow." Gunner said.

This information was literally blowing my mind. I knew I needed to get to the bottom of this shit because Aja didn't need this shit in her life right now.

"Hey y'all we need to keep this shit to ourselves until we really know what's going on. My sister doesn't need to know anything about this until we straighten it out." Ace said and I couldn't agree more.

"I hate to bring this up Ace but we can do a DNA test on Aja and April to see if they are related if you want me to. We can call Doc Murphy and have him put a rush on it." He said looking directly at Ace.

"Yeah man, do that shit. I don't care what the results say that's my sister. But, this shit got my head spinning. What the fuck is going on?" He asked.

My phone rang and I saw it was Tan.

"What's up Tan?" I answered.

"Man, I lost April. Her ass went into the bathroom and never came out. She must have snuck out the window." He said.

"Don't worry about it her ass will turn up just keep watching for her. Have you seen my Pops? They were together this morning." I said.

"Yeah, she left his house and I followed her to Outback. You want me to head over and check on him?" Tan asked.

"Yeah, do that man because some crazy shit is going down." I told him.

"Hey I think I found out some info on the club shooting. It seems some cat named Rick was one of the shooters. I couldn't see his face on the video from the club but somebody yelled out, "Rick come on!" towards the end of the shooting.

Does Ace have any beef with someone named Rick?" Tan asked.

I had him on speaker so Ace was already shaking his head no.

"Naw man we not even beefing with anyone right now. None of the cat's I have been dealing with goes by Rick." Ace answered.

"Well let me do some more digging and I will get back with y'all. Let me go check on your Pops and I will hit you back." He said hanging up.

"Do you think this Rick cat is the same one that shot Aja and Akia?" Ray asked.

"Could be we won't know until we figure out who this mutherfucker is."

I got a text from my chef saying he had everything set up outside for my late night date with Aja. I almost forgot about it with all the info that we were being hit with tonight. I text him confirming everything and hit Aja and let her know to be ready in an hour. I couldn't wait to see her because she always calmed me down. I just hated that I had all this information that I was keeping from her. But, it was all to protect her.

"So Gunner I need you to stay here for a while and work on getting us more information on April and Aja. I know you hate to be away from your crib but this is important. I will pay you extra and you can use the guest house to set-up and sleep. I also know how much you like your eyes so keep them to yourself when you see Aja." I said seriously.

Gunner was a ladies man. They all went crazy for him but that shit would get him killed fucking with mine. Ray busted out laughing.

"Ro you crazy as hell! He can't even look at her to say hi now?

I chose to ignore they ass. I was thinking about what our next move when I realized that Gunner was awfully quiet.

"I didn't scare your ass to bad did I Gunner?"
I asked.

He just shook his head and said, "Naw man just trying to get a game plan on where to look next for this info. "

"Wait a minute man you never did say the other thing you found." Ray said.

Gunner shifted nervously in his seat and looked at all of us.

"You know that saying don't shoot the messenger? Well, I'm going to need for y'all not to shoot my ass once I finish." He said and then everybody looked directly at me.

I had chuckled to myself.

"Naw man I ain't gonna shoot your ass. What is it that got you so shook?" I asked.

"I made sure to check all the information twice before I brought it to you all. The problem I found was what was on Ace's birth certificate." He said.

"Aw hell naw don't tell me my shit is fake too." Ace said.

"No it's not fake at all it's just that the name of your father on your birth certificate shocked me." He said with a weird look on his face.

"Man, Gunner it ain't no telling, you know April been around the block a few times. I never even looked at my birth certificate because I ain't ever needed to. Who's the deadbeat mutherfucker?" Ace said.

Gunner looked at all of us and said, "The name listed as your father is Rodney Casey. Ro and Raymond's dad.

Rodney

I got a call after April left the house saying that one of my shipments was jacked. Ace and Ray usually handled the drug part of the business but with them away I had to take care of it. I had to put off talking to the boys about Ace being their brother. I don't know how they are going to take it when I finally get down there and explain everything. I went to my office to make some phone calls to find out who was messing with my money and to also check on some missions that was going on. After sending out some emails and text I went upstairs to grab a beer and order some food.

As I was making my way towards the kitchen I suddenly felt a sharp pain at the back of my head and everything went black. I came to and I was chained to a pole in a room with boarded up windows. My hands were free but my right leg had a shackle around it tethered to the thick pole.

I knew I wasn't getting out of that anytime soon. I touched the back of my head because it was throbbing and felt a big knot at the back from where I had been hit. Somebody had stripped me down to just my boxers.

I looked around and saw they had placed a bottle of water and a bucket within walking distance of the chain. I knew I wasn't drinking that shit because it was no telling what was in it. I tried to figure out who had the balls to come in my house and snatch me. My house had a state of the art security system that I paid top money for. Hell, I used a military contractor to install it. No alarms had sound at all while I was downstairs, so I whoever took me, had to have known the code. The only people who knew it were Ro, Ray, Ace, and I. I looked at the door across the room but it was too far for me to reach with the chain on my leg.

I sat there and was trying to come up with a plan when I heard voices coming from another room. I tried to make out what they were saying but it all sound muffled. I could tell it was a man and a woman talking low. The voices sound familiar to me but i couldn't place them. I knew my boys would come and look for me soon because I always talked to them several times a day. I just had to figure out a way to survive until they came for me or I found a way out. I heard the knob jiggle on the door indicating someone was unlocking it. The light that came in when it opened temporarily blinded me. I heard footsteps coming towards me. Once my eyes adjusted, I looked up into the eyes of the last person I expected to see.

Chapter 15-April

I strutted in with a smile on my face looking down on his pathetic ass! He really thought I loved him. After I left I noticed I was being followed and called my brothers. Damon told me we had to move our timetable up in case someone had figured out what was going on. Rodney never gave me the code to his house but I knew it was his dead wife's birthday. Doug knocked Rodney out from behind and him and Damon put him in the trunk and brought him here.

Now he was chained like the dog he was. I couldn't wait for my man to get here so we could finally take care of him.

"Hey Lover!" I said with a smile.

I loved seeing the emotions playing across his face. There was hurt, shock, and anger all rolled into his eyes.

"You stupid bitch! You know I'm going to kill you when I get out of here right?" Rodney screamed.

"Awwww are your feelings hurt? Are you big mad or little mad?" I said taunting him with a smile on my face.

I could see his face turning redder by the minute and it made me smile even more.

"Why the fuck do you have me chained up April! I gave your hoe ass everything and this is how you treat me? We share a son together!" He said trying to play the baby daddy card.

"First of all Rodney there are so many things you have done to me to make me betray you. When we first met all those years ago before you got married I was the woman holding you down. I went against my brothers for you because I loved you. They wanted me to set you up but I was young and dumb back then. I was at the salon when Evette came in flashing that big ass diamond talking about y'all got married over the weekend. Which was funny because you failed to mention that the night before when you was face down between my legs? I was good enough to fuck but not marry." I said.

He looked at me funny and said,

"You knew I was in love with Evette and that she was pregnant when we started messing around. She was your best friend after all!" He said.

I looked at him and laughed again.

"Well, your precious Evette was fucking my brother! Doug is Raymond's father. She never loved you! She just wanted you for your money and power! She was funding my brother's lifestyle with your money! Those robberies at Big C's and your drug houses back in the day were all from information that your precious Evette provided." I said.

"Fuck you, April! I know you are lying! Evette wouldn't do that shit to me!" He said trying to lunge and get at me.

"Oh it's true alright. She was so sick of being with you that she wanted out. All she wanted to do was be with my brother and you couldn't stand it! That's why you killed her!" I shouted.

He immediately froze and tears started running down his face.

"Naw man I loved Evette I wouldn't do that to her!" He screamed.

I pulled out the recorder that I had and pressed play.

"Rodney, I can't be with you anymore! I am in love with someone else. I want a divorce!" Evette screamed.

Rodney stood there frozen looking at his wife as she spewed off those hateful words.

"Evette you can't leave me baby. I love you! We have two sons together! Why are you trying

to break our family apart?" He said trying to get
through to her.

She looked at Rodney and shook her head.

*"Rodney, Ro is grown and Raymond is not
even your biological child. I am done living with
someone that I don't love. Every time you touch
me I literally get sick to my stomach! I want to be
with my man!" Evette said.*

*"Rodney why are you looking at me like that!!
Get your hands off me! Rodney no I can't
breathe!" Evette said in a raspy voice.*

"Rodney's gone bitch! You got me now!" The
voice had gotten deeper than Rodney's normal
voice.

There were more noises of pain and crying as
Evette was beaten, raped, and murdered. There
were sounds of her taking her last breath. Then
you hear the strange voice again.

*"Nobody plays Rodney and me and gets away
with it!"*

You hear a door slam and the tape ends with screams from Ro as he finds his mom's dead body. I click the tape off and watch Rodney crumble to the ground.

"Well it looks like we know where Ro gets his temper from. She told me you were crazy but damn! You turned into a whole other person." I laughed as he broke down crying.

I turned around and strutted to the door and paused.

"Oh and by the way, Ace is not your son either." I went out the door laughing harder.

Breaking his ass down was only the first step of many in our plans. I couldn't wait for my man to get here so he could really break him down.

Rodney

I sat down on the cold floor a broken man. I couldn't believe that I was the one who killed my heart. I don't remember anything about that day but the call that I got from Raymond telling me to come home.

I had always had a bad temper and blackouts but my Dad told me not to worry about it. How was I going to explain to my sons that I killed their mama and don't even remember doing it? The tears were flowing down as I thought of the curse that I passed on to Ro. If I could kill my wife in cold blood what was Ro capable of?

I had to find a way out of here so I could get my son some help before it was too late. April thought she had hurt me more by saying Ace and Raymond weren't my sons but I already knew Ray was not mine biologically but it didn't matter to me I raised all three of them as my sons. I was still spinning from all the shit that

April told me about Evette. I couldn't believe she was working with the enemy all this time. Even though it hurt I still loved her. I prayed I got out of here soon because I had plans for that bitch April. She would die slowly and painfully for her part in this shit.

Tyesha

I had been stuck on this damn boat for a few days now and I was bored as hell. All Main wanted to do was get me to suck his dick and fuck me in my ass. I am so sick of this shit! I wanted to hurry up so I could get back to my girls and my man. Plus this mutherfucker was scaring the hell out of me.

I had went snooping in the room he was sleeping in and found all kinds of pictures of Aja from when she was a little girl until now. He also kept watching a video of her and him having sex. It looked like she was drugged out and out of it. Every time he watched it I knew i was going to be in for a world of hurt. He never had anything but oral or anal sex with me. He said he only wanted to be in Aja's pussy.

At this moment I was soaking in the tub because I literally couldn't sit down. We had watched Ro and his crew living it up at his beach house. Even though I had Derrick, I also considered Ro my man. It was really getting on my damn nerved watching him cater to her prissy ass when he treated me like shit. I don't know why all these men were so crazy for her ass. I decided to FaceTime Derrick and see what he was doing.

"Hey Bae where the kids at?" I asked as soon as his face came across the screen.

"They good they with your dad right now. He was getting mad that my Pops has them all the time." Derrick said.

"Okay make sure to give them a kiss from me once you pick them up. So did the plan work?" I asked.

Derrick and a few of his crew were planning to jack one of Ace's shipments that was coming in.

"Yeah baby, we got his money and his weed! I popped a few of his workers too for good measure too!" Derrick said with a big grin on his face.

"Baby, I am so proud of you! It's all coming together. TT and your daddy have Rodney stashed away so he's not in the picture. You can go ahead with the next phase and hit the rest of Ace's stash." I said.

"Word, I'll put the crew together. Has Main been treating you right down there?" Derrick asked.

There was no way I was telling Derrick I was fucking Main. He would go the fuck off. Plus my Uncle Damon said to keep it private when I was doing favors for him and Main. Ever since I had my girls Uncle Damon only ate my pussy. He said he was proud I bought his granddaughters into this world.

"You know how Main is. He doesn't say too much to me. He said he had a plan in the works that would pop off tomorrow." I said.

We talked for a little while longer going over the plan and had a little phone sex and I hung up. I was getting wrinkled sitting in the tub so I dried off and got ready for bed. As I was wrapping my hair there was a knock on the door. I knew it was Main so I said come in.

"Tyesha, I have everything set up for tomorrow so I need you to be ready. You have to keep him busy so I can snatch up Aja and we can hop on the jet and get home." Main said.

"Okay I can do that. My dad said he also had three couples lined up that want babies. He said that he will set-up the event for as soon as you get back." I told him.

He nodded his head and started texting on his phone. I kept getting ready for bed hoping he would leave me alone for one night. I knew that wouldn't be the case as soon as he pulled out the wig. He had a long wig that he would use when he wanted me to pretend to be Aja. I knew not to argue because he was known to have heavy hands. I have seen him beat my Aunt April black and blue. I put the wig on and made sure to make my eyes bigger. He turned the lights off and put the DVD in the player. It was the same video of him and Aja. I hated what was about to happen because Main was not a small man. He was very well endowed but didn't know how to be gentle.

"Aja baby I've missed you so much. I need you to come and suck on your dick. "He said in that creepy ass voice used when talking to her.

I got down on my knees and proceeded to do as he asked. Twenty minutes later he was leaving my room and I went to the bathroom to see the damage. He got mad while I was giving him head because I wasn't acting like Aja enough. He had rammed me so hard in the mouth that there was blood dripping out of it on each side. It also felt like my tooth was loose. With makeup and a little salt water I would be okay. It didn't do any good to complain about it. This was what I was trained to do. I was just thankful that all he wanted was head. I took care of my hygiene and went to bed. Hopefully by the end of the day tomorrow he would have the real Aja and leave me alone.

Main/Unknown

That bitch couldn't even act enough like Aja to get me off. I had to go back to my room and jack off to the tape of me making love to my angel for the first time. After finishing off in the shower for the second time I finished washing up and getting prepared for tomorrow. Rodney was taken care of now all I needed to do was to get Ro away from Aja so I could get her for good. I pulled out the ring box and looked at the flawless princess cut five carat diamond ring I had made for my queen. The matching band was being prepared as we speak with diamonds all around the band. Its inscription read, "Forever mine". I couldn't wait to marry her and drop my seeds in her. I found out that she miscarried our first born. I hated that she had to go through that without me. But, it would be okay because we had plenty of time to make lots of babies.

I also couldn't wait to get back to Nashville to get my revenge on Rodney. He tried to kill me once before but failed. He didn't know that of course. I had to text Damon and Doug to also go ahead and set-up the event. We had some couples that would be bidding on a baby that we had snatched from Louisiana. A little girl that I knew would bring us a cool million or two. We had events as we called them at least twice a week. I had to make sure that I had enough money stacked to take care of my queen and our offspring. I couldn't wait for tomorrow to get here so I could have her all to myself. As long as everything went according to plan I didn't see a problem. I didn't want to hurt anybody just yet but if anyone got in the way of him getting his angel it would be lights out.

Chapter 16-Aja

I was so excited I didn't know what to do. Every time I thought about Ro I would get butterflies in my stomach. He treated me like I was the most precious thing on Earth and I must admit I was loving every minute. He always said he didn't know how to be a good boyfriend but what he didn't know was that I loved all his quirks. Everybody kept telling me that Ro was crazy and yes I could see that he was different but so was I.

Living years in isolation and fear had made me go crazy. There would be days that I would be so depressed that I considered taking my life several times. I figured everyone would be safe if I was dead. I would be able to escape him and hurt him by taking away the one thing he truly wanted which was me. Kyra made me go see someone after she caught me staring at a bottle of Percocet's. After talking to the therapist he said I had severe Depression. I went to counseling and have a slew of pills I take just to help me stay sane. I just happened to be good at covering up my problems.

Ace had signed us up for all kinds of self-defense classes and had us at the gun range every week. He wanted to make sure I was prepared for the next time that my stalker attacked.

I looked in my closet and chose a sheer white top and a white bodycon strapless dress to go up under it. Ro told me we would be on the beach so I chose a pair of simple flip flops to slide on. I decided not to wear any underwear because you would definitely see the lines with the way the dress was hugging my curves. I sprayed on some Daisy by Marc Jacobs and put on a little bit of MAC lip gloss to make my lips pop. I headed downstairs and Ro was waiting for me at the bottom of the stairs.

He looked so good in his simple white tank showing his muscles and the one tattoo he had of a viper on his arm. He had on some white linen shorts and was barefoot. He looked me over like I was a meal he wanted to eat; I smiled as he licked those plump lips that did things to my body that should be illegal. He grabbed my hand and led me out to the beach. I looked at the water's edge and noticed candles in the shape of a heart surrounding a blanket with a bottle of champagne, fruit, cheese and ham cubes, and some type of chocolate mousse. He led me over and I sat down pulling my legs underneath me.

"Ro wow this is amazing! I can't believe you did all of this." I said.

He smiled a smile I had never seen from him before. It was a carefree and playful smile. It had me grinning from ear to ear.

"I tried for you baby girl. This shit really ain't me. I ain't even gonna front. I had to look on Google for ideas." He said.

We both laughed and started filling the small plates with food to munch on. Ro poured us both a glass of champagne and we sipped and watched the wave's crash in front of us.

"Ro I know we just met but I have to admit that I'm falling for you. I don't want you to say anything back I just felt like you should know how I feel." I said getting it out all in one breath.

He stared at me for a while and then looked off across the water. He took a breath and grabbed my hand.

"Baby girl, you don't know how it makes me feel to hear you say that. But, I'm not sure if I'm good enough for you. There's a lot of stuff about me that you don't know. I'm not the good guy or knight in shining armor shit you read about in them books. I'm flawed like a mutherfucker and I'm not sure if I can change that." He said.

"Ro I don't care how flawed you are. I'm far from perfect, believe me. I barely hold it together to get up some days. I know what my brother does for a living so I know you are in the streets in some type of capacity. As long as you treat me right and accept me for my flaws I can rock with you." I told him looking into his eyes so he could see how serious I was.

"Aja I kill people for a living. I have killed over a hundred people and I don't feel the least bit bad about it. I enjoy doing it. It gives me a rush that's almost as good as being in some pussy. How can you love someone like that? I'm a fucking monster!" He shouted.

I looked at him and saw the pain in his eyes. I got up and straddled him and put my hands on either side of his face staring into his eyes.

"If you are a monster than you can be my monster. I know you would never hurt me because you show me how much you care every day. I have never felt safe with anyone except for you. Maybe you don't see it but you are a protector and that's why you are good at what you do." I said.

He grabbed me and kissed me hard. We both tumbled back onto the blanket. He lifted up my skirt and groaned when he realized I wasn't wearing any underwear. He slipped his fingers in my folds and felt how wet I was. He was driving me crazy and I just wanted him inside of me.

"Ro please!" I said almost screaming it.

He unzipped his shorts and pulled his third leg out and before I could catch my breath he had filled me to capacity. It felt like he was in my chest! He was hitting my g-spot over and over again so hard you could hear his skin hitting up against my skin. All the raw energy that he possessed seemed to be in every stroke.

"Come ride me." He said in between strokes.

He flipped us over without pulling out. I slowly slid up his pole until only the tip was in and slammed back down and repeated the motion again. Ro's eyes were closed and his head was thrown back in ecstasy. I felt a delicious tingle letting me know that I was close to cumming. I started going faster chasing the feeling that only Ro could give me. He grabbed my waist and started meeting my thrust and causing the pressure to become unbearable.

"Oh shit Aja! Baby girl cum with me!" He commanded. His tone sent me over the edge and I almost fainted from cumming so hard. Ro picked up the pace and I felt thick ropes of his seeds filling me up. This sent me into another orgasm. I collapsed on his chest after the feeling subsided. We lay there for a few minutes trying to catch our breath.

"Aja I know I should let you go but I can't. I have to have you near me at all times. I just need you to know that I'm possessive as hell when it comes to you. I don't even like Ace being too close to you. I literally see red when any man is near you. I don't want to scare you but I need you to know what you're dealing with when it comes to me. I have an anger problem that's hard to control. I have blackouts where I can't remember what the hell I have done." Ro said.

I thought about what I could say to put him at ease. I figured maybe I should share some of my secrets too.

"I have severe Depression and thought about killing myself after what happened to Tyler. I blamed myself for his death because he was killed because of me. I have counseling sessions and I take pills to help me sleep and keep my depression at bay. I have panic attacks sometimes and I am very paranoid. Can you deal with my flaws?" I said rubbing his chest.

He sat up and looked at me and smiled.

"So what you are saying is you crazy as hell too!" He said and we both laughed.

"Naw baby girl, real talk circumstances have you messed up. I was born like this. I went to the head doctors and they told me I'm real messed up. They said I have several things wrong with me. I'm Bipolar with psychotic tendencies. I also have borderline split personality disorder. I'm afraid of what I do when I have my black outs. I don't want you to get hurt." Ro said with a worried expression on his face.

I wasn't expecting him to tell me he suffered from the various mental issues that he listed. I can't lie and say I wasn't worried but it was a part of him that I would accept because it made him who he was.

" How about we take it one day at a time so you can see that I'm not going anywhere. I just want you to give me a chance, Ro." I said.

He was still staring out into the water but his shoulders relaxed a little more.

"I just knew you would walk away once you heard my secrets." He said pulling me in his arms. I laughed and snuggled into him.

"I'm not going anywhere except maybe to take a shower. I have sand in places that I shouldn't.

He chuckled and helped me up so we could get dressed.

"Come on baby girl, I can help wash some of those areas for you." He whispered in my ear.

I smiled and grabbed his hand as we walked back up the beach. After, making love in the shower we lay in his bed and watched old episodes of Martin. It felt so good to just relax and chill with him. I wanted our night to last forever. Just as I was about to fall asleep I felt a chill run down my spine. Ro must have felt me shudder because he pulled me in closer to him.

"You cold baby girl?" He asked.

"Maybe a little. I said.

He pulled me closer and I laid my head on his chest. I got an awful feeling in my stomach that something bad was about to happen. I just prayed that all the people I loved would be okay.

Unknown/Main

I watched as Ro took advantage of my angel. I had gotten up to get a drink of water and saw the flickering light on the beach. I got out my binoculars and watched as he fucked her. Nobody was supposed to touch her but me! I had to get her tomorrow before he could take her from me! I was pissed the fuck off and someone had to pay!

I went downstairs to Tyesha's room and kicked in the door. She started screaming. Before she could utter another word I punched her in her mouth. I started beating and kicking her everywhere until she stopped moving. I needed her to scream and feel my pain. I yanked off her panties and threw her on the bed. I rammed my dick so far up her ass that I felt blood running all over my dick. She woke up and started crying and screaming again.

"Shut up bitch!" I said punching her in her mouth.

I continued to ram into her. I was taking out all my anger and rage on her and I didn't give a fuck. When I felt myself about to cum I pulled out and rammed myself in her mouth and came. After I pulled out I punched her and knocked her ass out again. I was still mad but that took the edge off. I told her what would happen if she let another man touch her. She would learn to listen to me or people would suffer. I would start with her sister Kia. My plan had to change since Tyesha wouldn't be available to distract Ro. I would just have to be creative. I was trying to spare Ro but since he felt the need to touch what was mine. He had to die!

Chapter 17-Ro

I woke up the next morning with the sun beating on my face and a soft body wrapped around me. I couldn't believe that I slept through the night without any nightmares. I looked down and moved the hair out of Aja's face. She was so beautiful and I couldn't help but smile thinking about last night. She accepted me with all my flaws and hadn't even flinched when I told her about my problems. She didn't judge me for being a killer. I would try and make this work with us because I know I couldn't let her go now if I wanted to. She was my calm and light from the darkness in my soul.

I eased out of bed and went to handle my hygiene. While I was brushing my teeth I saw a text from Pops saying he was coming after all today to talk to me. I texted him back and said alright I would stick around and wait on him. I couldn't wait for him to meet my lady. Yeah, I was claiming her! I'd be a fool not to. I was planning on taking her out today somewhere special to let her know how I felt about her. I had never been in love before but I could tell that I was falling fast for her. I went in the closet and threw on some Nike sweatpants and a matching tank so I could make my baby some breakfast. I kissed her on her forehead before I made my way downstairs to cook.

Ace, Kyra, Kia, Gunner and Ray were all downstairs around the kitchen island talking.

"Hey bro you gonna cook breakfast this morning?" Ray's hungry ass asked.

"Yeah I got you, give me a minute to get everything ready." I said getting everything out.

I looked in the fridge and saw what I had. I decided I would make bacon, cheese eggs, and peach Belgian waffles. As I started cooking Gunner told us he had some more information. I told him it was okay to talk in front of the girls. It was time to let everyone know what was going on. Too much shit was going down without them being prepared. I told Kia to go and wake up baby girl.

Thirty minutes later I was putting platters of food on the table and Aja was coming down. She had on one of my shirts and a pair of PINK yoga pants. Her cute little feet were bare. Even in something so simple she took my breath away. She came over with a smile and kissed me. I grabbed her and just held on.

"Ummm the pregnant woman is hungry and i want to eat." Kia said making everyone laugh.

We all sat down at the patio table and started eating. We had Gunner fill the girls in on everything that was going on. They all sat shocked at what was being revealed.

"So who the hell am I if you can't find a birth certificate? And Ace, Ray, and Ro are brothers?

This is fucked up!" Aja said and I couldn't blame her.

This was some Jerry Springer shit.

"Well I have some answers but I don't have them all." Gunner said.

"We ran April's prints and found out that her real name is Giselle Waters. The thing is Giselle Waters was kidnapped when she was three years old. I am looking into finding her family so I can get some more information. Doc Murphy also ran the DNA between April and Aja. April is not her biological mother. We are waiting to hear back about Ace's DNA results." Gunner said.

We all turned to look at Aja. I grabbed her hand as she wiped away tears with the back of her hand.

"I can't believe this shit! How can she do this to me?" She cried.

Ace and Kia came over and hugged her.

"I don't care what that paper says. You are always going to be my little sister." Ace said with tears in his eyes.

"That's not all I found out. The way the records were altered let me know that it was someone that had done this before. I think.......

POW POW POW!!!!!

Glass started shattering all around us. I dived on Aja and pulled her under the table. I looked around and saw that Gunner had been hit. The rest of us were under the table ducking. Shots were still being fired with chunks of marble flying everywhere.

"We have to get the girls out of here!" Ray said.

I knew he was worried even more since Kia was pregnant.

"Gunners hit! We need to get him out of here too. Ace and Ray you take the range and get Kia and Gunner out of here. I will cover you." I said.

I had six guns tapped under the table. We quickly retrieved them and started firing back.

"Aja, Kyra, and I will be right behind you!" I shouted over the sound of bullets.

We all nodded our heads in agreement and they took off towards the garage with gunner thrown over Ace's shoulder. Aja and I shot in the direction of the shooters to cover them while Kyra crawled towards the garage. We heard tires screeching so I was guessing they made it. I pulled out my cell phone and logged into my security system. I saw that there were six shooters surrounding the house. I watched as a black Hummer pulled up and started shooting them one by one. I looked out and saw my Pops getting out of the truck.

"Baby girl it's okay. My Pops just pulled up and took care of the rest of them. Go get Kyra." She shook her head yes and took off.

I went towards the front door and unlocked it so he could come in. I heard Kyra and Aja talking so I headed back towards the kitchen to make sure they were okay. Behind me I heard the door open and yelled back for Pops to follow me. When I got back to the kitchen the girls were standing by the island talking.

"Baby girl I want you to meet my Pops Rodney." Aja turned around with a smile on her face holding her hand out to shake his.

"Hi my angel. I told you I would come for you." Pops said.

I watched Aja start breathing fast and shaking. Tears started falling and urine ran down her leg.

"Pops what the fuck are you talking about?" I said turning around to look at him.

He pulled out a gun and shot Kyra and turned the gun on me. I felt a burning in my chest and instantly got nauseous. Aja was screaming and trying to wake up Kyra. He walked over to me and kneeled down. He looked just like my Pops but then I noticed that there was a scar across his neck like someone had tried to slit his throat.

"It's nice to meet you nephew! Sorry we had to meet under these circumstances but I just couldn't let you have what was mine. He raised the gun and fired my world instantly turned black…………..

To Be Continued

HAVE YOU READ
THIS?

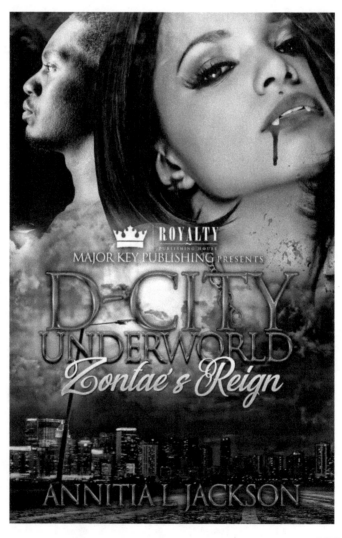

About The Author:

Annitia was born in Nashville, Tennessee and was raised by her loving grandparents Hattie and Ernest. She discovered her love for writing in the 5th Grade thanks to a wonderful teacher named Ms. Middlebrooks. She has written stage plays, television scripts, short stories, and now novels. Annitia has been married to the love of her life Ron and they share a handsome five-year-old son named Nathaniel. She lives overseas and loves to read, travel, and dance.

Note from the Author:

Thank you for reading the first book in the D-City Chronicles series! I appreciate you so much for taking the time to read something that is near and dear to my heart. I am currently working on part two so stay tuned. Please leave a review on Amazon. As a new author in this literary world, I'm encouraged by your reviews and your willingness to read and hopefully enjoy my work.

I am always available to hear your comments and opinions. I love you ALJ readers!!!!

Website: www.annitialjackson.com

Facebook:
https://www.facebook.com/DCityChronicles/?ref
=aymt_homepage_panel#

Instagram: https://www.instagram.com/anniti
aljackson/

Twitter:
https://twitter.com/ANNITIALJACKSON

Here are a list of Book Club discussion questions provided by my reading crew:

1. We now know a little more about Tyesha's origins and the "family" dysfunction she was brought up in. Is Tyesha i a villain or a victim?

2. In the African American community, seeking help for mental health issues is considered taboo. In what ways has this stigma driven the events of the story?

3. Do you think Aja moved to fast by having sex with after knowing him only for a day?

4. What secret do you think Kyra is keeping?

5. Who is Ace's real father?

6. Was Aja kidnapped?

7. Why didn't Rodney and Ro know their father was a twin?

8. Where did April get that tape, and will she use it in the future, ex. blackmail?

9. What are your feelings about marrying your cousin?

10. Are Ro and Kyra dead?

Be sure to <u>LIKE</u> our Major Key Publishing

page on Facebook!

CPSIA information can be obtained
at www.ICGtesting.com
Printed in the USA
BVHW042239230320
575807BV00011B/908